BEING YOUNG CAN BE DANGEROUS

COUGER

When Your Being Haunted

A Novel

Billie Dureya Shell

COUGER

Front Cover Image By graphic designer Billie
Dureyea Shell & Kenny Writes

First Printing Edition 2021

ISBN 9781737392217

Team Shell

ACKNOWLEDGEMENT

First and foremost I have to give honor to My Lord And Saviour Jesus Christ without him now of this would be possible. 2020 was a MUTHA FUCCA Corona Virus made shit hard 4 niggas but we made it threw y'all keep your head up and know that God got us, no matter they throw in our way no one can stop what God has plan for you...
Its 2021 now FUCC 2020 and Covid 19.... Now to my family momma I love you and you no I got you no matter what. You mean the world 2 me oh and NO MORE PINCHING LOL.
To my little sister Glenda I love you blackie, you No I Got You always

To my Wife Shatoya Shell you get on my damn nerves 👰 but I wouldnt trade you 4 anything In the world I love 🖤 you more then words can ever express. To all my children 👶👶 I love y'all Jazmine, Ant'Tuan, Davon, Anthony, David, Lil Dureyea, Alura, Queen Diavion, Cameron, Preniece, Shaniece and Tajh I love u all and I'll 4ever have ur back you all give me a reason 2 smile... to my cousin Zane RIP nigga I miss u more then anyone will ever no, your always remembered love you bro. to my cousin Ty I miss you thank 4 looking out 4 me and Zane you played a big part in my life and I always looked up to you I love you... Uncle Woody I miss you and love you, you no your my favorite uncle... To my nigga Jamal love you, my brothers Lawrence and fred thank 4 showing me the game I love yall 4 that. To my oldest sister Nedra love you thank you 4 always having my back. to my family uncles anties cousins etc.. I love y'all even those of you that act funny as fuck

To my dark side niggas y'all no what it is YAAH GANG....
Now to all my readers and fans I love you thanks for reading I
hope u enjoy this book as much as I enjoy writing
them with this Corona Virus 19 shit there ain't shit to do but
write so I'm on my shit with that being said y'all be safe cover
your face and love each other life is short so love the ones that
really love I'm gone no. enjoy the book

STAY SAFE

Author Billie Dureyea Shell

THERE'S NOTHING U CANNOT DO
IF U PUT UR MIND 2 IT.

All you nigga's got EDD money so aint no excuse
why you can't get a book LOL

CHAPTER 1

The name's Taylor James, I'm forty-eight and I gets mines; be it dick, dollars or more dick ya heard. Some call me an old freak cause dis snappers lethal and can't no dude with wrinkly balls and grey nut hair do her right. A fine bitch of my caliber can pass for twenty-five and I don't fucks nothing over it ya heard. I especially like dem young ones, babbyyy! Ump, dem young big dick bastards can fuck for hours ya heard me! Shit, my pussy wet just thinking bout it. Anywhoo, I live in Hartford's north end in this project called Nelton Court. There's about a hundred and fifty two-floored apartments with a tiny slab of concrete that couldn't be considered a porch or a stoop; but I'd cop a squat and watch the happs until something or somebody caught my eye. And let me tell you, Nelton always had something happening, take last night for instance... This crackhead name Shelly was on the side of building seventy givin'

Omar a dick suck for a quick fix. She waited 'til Omar's eyes were rollin' and his knees were quivering like a virgin bout to get eleven inches for her first time, when she bit down on his six inches. That's a snack to me, I'd gobble dick and balls like bam! Anywhoo, Shelly snatched up Omar's sac of heroin and took off thru the courts, bobbin' and weavin'. Thinkin' her ass made a getaway she stopped, leaned against the building, opened the lil glassine bag and wham! Omar hit her ass in the back with a lil Louie slugger. Her ass hit the ground, mouth wide, takin' in grass and dirt while the stolen heroin drifted in the air like softly falling snow. Hilarious! I laughed so hard my side hurt, tears fell and I thought I'd pee myself. So here I sat, watchin' kids wait on the school bus for their last two weeks of school before summer vacay started. Dem lil mafuckas kept shit goin too; fightin' over these hot pussy girls, while the girls climbed out windows and snuck off to grind at a house party. And yeah, I do those too; if it's a party, Taylor James is up in there, I don't discriminate feel me. Shit, last week I crashed eight year-old Timmy's party. His momma Brenda couldn't stand my ass and the feeling's mutual; (I fucked her baby daddy Chocolate, the same day he got out) bet her ass ain't step to me and ask me to leave neither. Smirk. So I'm chillin' then feel my eyes widen, my retinas expand and my jaw drops when Toni's ass gets outta Brick's car; but not before swappin' spit, Brick is her sister Kelly's man. Now these two scandalous bitches weren't identical twins, so this was not a case of mistaken identity. Ump, I smacked my lips and filed that info away for later. Toni switched up the cracked, uneven sidewalk and almost bussed her ass when her heel got stuck in-between. To piss her off I started laughing, burning cig dangling between my pouty, succulent lips. "Damn girl, you a'ight?" I asked all sincere like I gave two fucks; and givin' up two of those is a rare damn thang! Toni glared, trying to figure out if I was being legit, then said, "Yeah, I'm sure yo ass would've come to my rescue." all flippant and shit. See, that's why I don't do kids boo, cause they always gotta try you. Your kids or not, but I'd stomp 'em into next week like they mines. "Girl you know I gotchu, you my peeps." I glanced up the street and could see Brick at the light, his right turn signal blinking. "Where's Kelly?" Toni stared at me, as if contemplating what to say and how far to take shit. The fire dimmed in her violet colored contacted eyes. "I'll see you later Taylor, gotta get ready for school. I'll tell mom dukes you said hi." My smile grew. "You do that and while you're at it, tell her ass I need my fifty dollars." Toni's superior look fell, side stepping me she entered their apartment to my right. Cigarette finished, I chucked it into my neighbor Vicki's rose bush, stood, dusted off my ass and decided to walk down to the corner store for some snacks. Manny's bodega, Red Star restaurant and a closed dry cleaners sat on one corner, followed by apartment buildings. Across the street sat their competition, a twenty-four hour corner store called Simply Twenty Four and a small soul food eatery called Hot Pots. I hadn't tried too much from there, but what I'd had; cabbage, white rice and porgies was good. They were just hella expensive, so I ate there when a nigga was trying to impress, not that it did. So fuck outta here thinkin' I'm a cheap bitch; ain't shit cheap over here, not even my drawers. Not feeling like fighting traffic just to go to the twenty-four cause niggas and bitches too drove like they were straight retarded; along with having no sight, 'cause every week somebody was crashing their shit. Last week a car full coming from a concert at the West was flyin' down North Main, lost control and slammed into the package store down Main; killing the front seat passenger and the backseat as well, while the driver walked off with a broken arm. Loud Spanish music greeted me upon entering Manny's, my hips automatically swayed to the beat. I could feel Manny's eyes on my hips, so I gave an ass shake, then headed for the snack aisle. I always craved sweets no matter if I smoked or not, one couldn't tell to look at me. I stood only five four with smooth, flawless dark chocolate skin, perfectly arched brows, pert nose, full lips, dimpled cheeks and almond shaped hazel eyes. I had full 38B breasts with tiny succulent nipples, a taut belly and curvy hips. What I didn't have was a big ole ghetto booty, I had a lil junk in the trunk and knew how to work it. Truthfully I wanted some ass shots, so I was saving my coins to have it done right. No way I'm goin' cheap and end up with one cheek bigger or lumpier than the other. "Hola senorita Tay-lore, do you need any help?" Sang Manny while mangling my damn name. Pasting on a smile, I grabbed two ninety-nine cent chips, one regular and one bbq flavor, turned and gave Manny a wink, "Hey Manny, nah boo I'm good," Turning back to the chips and whatnot, I grabbed a pack of six Oreo cookies, then sashayed up to the register for some candy. Out the corner of my eye I could see Manny's son Louis grillin' me all hard, so I purposely dropped a bag of chips, then got my eagle on; bounced a cheek, came up, looked over my shoulder and winked. Louis started flappin' his gums in Spanish, I knew it was about my black ass but oh fuckin' well. Don't be mad that you blew yo whole income tax check on me and ain't even get a gander at the panties. Yo fault boo. "Chu look very nice today Tay-lore." gushed Manny who then yelled something to Louis. All I caught was 'callate', which I knew mean shut up. "Yes, please shut the fuck up with yo hatin' ass." I thought with a devilish smile on my face. "Thanks boo, you don't look bad yoself." I flirted, although that was nothin' but lies, 'cause Manny had to weigh like three seventy five. He was baldin' but still stubbornly held onto tufts of hair he combed over his baldin' pale, bushy brows that damn near hid hazy black eyes. A wide, flat nose and thin lips that hid a mouth full of teeth so spaced out I wondered how his ass could eat anything. Manny cheesed and fumes of pickled pigs feet and bananas slapped me in the face, 'Uh let me get the usual." Manny eagerly grabbed two Paydays, a plain M&M and original sunflower seeds, then tallied it up. 'Five twenty-five Taylore." I handed over six, took my change, bag, walked out and exhaled, 'Damn dat Spick's breath was tart! Smelled like his ass munched on a thousand unwashed twats." I shuddered in mock horror. 'Yo! Yo Taylor! C'mere for a second!" I heard a voice yell. Glancing around I finally noticed Jermaine sitting in his F-150 waving. Rolling my eyes, I started to keep it movin', cause Taylor James don't do undercovers. Lickin' my lips I walked over to see what his tootie fruity fresh n fruity ass wanted. 'What nigga?" I coldly snapped, eying Jermaine's tan cargo shorts, boat shoes and plain white tee. His low haircut was minus any waves and cut high up on the sides. Jermaine wasn't an ugly dude, he just tried too hard to be something he's not, straight. 'Damn shorty, why you so cold to a nigga, I just wanna take you out to dinner. You like to eat don't chu?" 'Damn sure do, on dicks that aren't shoved up another dude's ass!" I wanted to yell, alerting the whole block to his charade. 'Duh, yeah I like to eat fool." I said instead. 'Well hop in, let's hit up the Chowder Pot," My lips curled 'cause I swear I smelled ass juice on his breath. 'Nah, maybe another time." Jermaine rolled his eyes, now what dude you know does that? "Yo ass been brushing me off for months, one day I'm a say fuck yo stuck up ass." He snapped, feelin' some type all in his voice. "Uh, uh, and when dicks fly you'll knock my ass out the way and be the first in line." "Well hell, do you boo. A bitch said not today and yo ass gets all in yo feelings an shit." I snapped ready to go off on his ass 'cause I don't owe his ass jack shit. Nigga think cause he got a few boosters on the team he all that. Not! His ass needs to go bend it over, get plugged and leave me the fuck alone! We eyed each other a moment, then Jermaine started his truck, revved the engine, pulled off without checking the mirror and smashed into a police car. Laughing, I watched Jermaine scramble to locate driver's license and car registration. Done with his ass, I turned and headed back to the courts. By three the courts were live, a basketball game started. As the game progressed a few shirts came off, allowing my eyes to drink in the splendor of hard, sweaty backs. Umm, a bitch pussy twitch at the sight of a cobra back, nice pecs and those six packs. Lorda mercy in Jesus name I pray, can I see da dick print, hallelujah, amen! Dozens of young, dumb hoes pushin' strollers with another cookin' in the oven like the shit was cute, were walkin' around in groups. Kids ran around makin' their own entertainment, a few stood with wine coolers or something harder in hand. "Sup Taylor, got an extra cig?" Asked Toni and Kelly's mom Rosalie. Now how the hell can you have an extra cigarette? That's like askin' for an extra titty, or an extra deep pussy. "Fifty cents." I held my hand out. "What?" Rosalie asked, confusion in her eyes. "Loosies cost fifty cents. 'Cause I know you, I won't charge my usual dollar. So you want a loosie, fifty cents." I broke it down for her slow ass. Well she wasn't really slow, but since she wanted to play like she was by not understanding what I said, I played along. I started to throw some sign language in the mix, even though I ain't know any. I hate dumb bitches. Rosalie rolled her eyes. Was it roll your eyes day and nobody told me? She smacked her big dick suckers. Shits so big she can whisper in her own damn ear; lips so big she can suck a dick from around the corner. I laughed to myself. "You're serious?" "As a heart attack. Picture me passin' out free cigs like govment cheese. Then when my shit done will I be able to get a cig from you? No. Will I be able to go to the store and buy a few more? No. Why? Since I'm broke 'cause I didn't charge for my cigs." I stressed. "Girl stop fuckin' playin' and give me a damn cig." Rosalie snapped, hand on hip. I stood up cause if Rosalie tried to jump bad, I'd punch her dead in them joints. My fist would most likely disappear, but I'd take that chance. "Hoe did you not hear what da fuck I just said? No bitch, now what!" "Girl whateva, keep yo ole raggedy ass cigs. It don't make no sense to be so selfish over something that costs fifty damn cents." She tartly stated. Was big lips serious? Selfish..... moi? Nah her ass couldn't be talkin' to the bitch who constantly lets her ass get eggs, cups of milk and toilet paper like I'm the damn twenty-four hour. And let's not forget her ass borrowed fifty motha-fuckin-dollars last month and had yet to pay a bitch back. "Listen Rosalie, are you listening?" Rosalie nodded. "Yes Taylor, even though you on the bullshit." With that, I drew back and slapped her ass so quick, so hard, spittle flew from her mouth. "Run me my fifty bitch; and as long as yo lips stay the size of a newborns ass, don't ever step to me all crazy." I didn't yell, cause wasn't no need to kick it up a ghetto notch. A Shocked look upon her face, dis hoe grew some balls, reached for my pack and crunched my joints. Oh no dis grandiose lip bitch didn't! Flippin' the ghetto switch, I stomped on dem corns and bunions Rosalie called feet, punched her ass in the stomach and when she bent over, gave a knee to the face; down she went! Glaring at her ass I kicked her a few times, patted her down like Officer Webster had done me numerous times and came across fifty bucks tucked in her bra. I snatched it and gave her another hearty kick to the ribs since she did the shit to herself. Like I said before, I hate dumb bitches. "Thanks hoe, I was broke. Tah tah," I taunted, turned and headed up the street to Barbour and the closest liquor store. Blue's package store, or as the hood called it, beg central, had the normal beggers on standby; from "Can you spare some change?", to "You got a car, I can fix it out back?". A chick name Omaide, who at one time thought she was the shizz nick, had joined the beggar crew and was offering up dick sucks, a quick fuck and an around the world special. Shaking my head, I stepped inside and groaned at the seven people ahead of me; all being held up cause some old lady was playing the daily numbers and sucked my teeth. Looking behind the Plexiglass, I could see only Cleotus' pervert ass workin', which meant the line would continue to move extra slow. Fuck! Then I spotted the helium voiced chick Sable three people ahead of me, yapping her mouth on her cell. Her ass should've been called Rat, 'cause Sable's ass was so ugly she put the U in that shit. I will admit, niggas flocked cause she was built like a brick shit house. I know niggas hit dat shit from the back, or put bags over her head so they wouldn't throw up. "Fuck it," I told myself and walked up on Sable. Sable Marie was around twenty-two and as far as I know her ass didn't have kids. Word was her womb was as fucked up as her face, which said a lot. Sable was banana yellow and her face was covered in freckles. Freckles are supposed to be cute right? Wrong, cause her joints were joined by big ass hairy moles that waved whenever a breeze kicked up. One of her eyes sat slightly lower than the other and didn't move or blink, so the mafucka ran continuously; which she'd dab with a colored head scarf. Her nose was thin, but her nostrils were wide and stuck in the flaring position. Even her lips were mis-matched, the upper fuller than the Bologna thin bottom. She did have some nice thick hair, which Sable kept done with weekly hair appointments. I eyed her ensemble, skin tight Red Monkey jeans and wifebeater tied with a knot in the back. I had to give Sable credit cause the outfit looked good, damn good. 'Hey Sable girl, how you doin'? Long time no see." I said in my 'we cool, happy to see you' voice. Sable smiled and I bit back a grimace. Oh yeah, her choppers were fucked up too, she had a bunch of extra joints and all of 'em were crooked as hell. 'Oh, heyy Taylor." she leaned in for a hug smelling of Valentino and Black & Mild's. 'How you been girl?" At first, I started to say some slick shit cause that's just me, but I reeled it in and toned it down when the line started to move. 'Good, good, what's been up with you girl?" Yawn. Like I gave two fucks. 'The usual, workin' and gankin' these niggas out they dough." My eyebrow arched. 'Work? Where you work at?" 'Down at Boobz, ain't no shame in my game girl. Yep, I strip and I'm also one of the headliners Thursday thru Sunday; the money's good." 'Word?" Sable nodded, stepped up to the window and gave her order. 'Maybe one day I'll stop by and see yo show." She cheesed. 'Great!" Sable reached inside her red Birken bag, pulled out a card, twenty dollars, paid for her liquor, Blacks, cigs and bounced. The card read 'Boobz: propertier Mason Albert Admission: price varies Thurs-Sun headliners: Silk, Candycane and Mink.' I stuck it in my pocket, gave my order and shot up the middle finger to the mad mafuckas that witnessed me cut the line. 'Let me get a Corona, a nip of peach Paul and a pack of Newport 100's." 'Grr." Cleotus growled, lustfully eying me through the Plexiglas. 'Hey sexy." Cleotus leaned down and whispered through an opening big enough to grab your purchases. 'If you stick around I'll take a fifteen-minute break; we can go in the stock room for a lil fun." he wiggled his eyebrows. 'Eww nigga, you done lost yo everlastin' mind. Do I look like one of yo easy lays for drink? Pst, ain't enough cash in the register for you to even look at this pretty ass snatch. Now give me my shit so I can go nigga!" I lashed out. People behind me laughed and clowned Cleotus who got pissed, threw my items, change and yelled out he was going on break. One dude kicked the door, another punched the Plexiglas. Best believe I bounced before they blamed me for that shit.

CHAPTER 2

"Hello, house of beauty and juicy pussy. How may I direct yo call?" was how I answered my phone. Dove burst out laughing. "Girl yo ass a lunatic, why you answerin' the phone like dat?" Chuckled Dove. Now Dove was this broad I sometimes kicked it with. She lived further down Main Street in a complex called Mary Shepard and yes, Dove's really her name. Either her momma had a thing for birds, the soap, whatever. I personally think its cause her ass looks like a damn bird; tall, skinny, gangly legs and a long ass pointy bird like beak, I mean nose. I swear her ass could wear a size one but she claimed a three adamantly. "Hoe, I pay the phone bill so until you do I'll answer as I damn well please, now what's up?" "Well damn, who jerked off in yo oatmeal?" Teeth suck. "Dove don't make me read yo ass. You know damn well a bitch don't waste skeet juice; its good for the body, like milk."

Dove laughed so hard her ass started choking. I pulled the receiver from my ear cause I ain't need to hear a whole bunch of chokin' and gaspin' for air. 'Damn!" Dove finally wheezed out, 'I could've been chokin' to death and yo ass just chillin'." I snorted. "Then you should've hung up and dialed 911 hoe; cause dis ain't da 'I'm chokin' what do I do?' hotline." Dove sighed. "Girl I can't with you. Anyway, you going out tonight? I hear the Bushnell got Shaggy performing." Shaggy hunh? I could definitely go Boombastic on dat dick, have Shaggy's fine ass Dancing and Shouting, while hollerin' Luv me luv me I need your love. 'Hell yeah, come scoop me on your way and be on time Dove." I told her always running late ass. "Okay, okay, let me go. Jeffrey's bad ass chewin' on my blunt." She hung up and I shook my head. Jeffrey was her bad ass, three year-old son. I remember one time while over her house, I told his lil ass to leave my drink alone. His bad ass gone tell me, 'shut the hell up 'cause I can hold my liquor.'. And when I asked who he think he's talkin' to he says, 'Do you see anybody else in here? I'm talkin' to yo bitch ass." And when I told Dove, her ass laughed and told me Jeff had a slick mouth. Babyy, I wanted to rough his lil shitty, still wearing diapers at three ass up! Anyway, enough bout Dove and her man child. Swallowing my Corona I decided to pick out my outfit early, strode into my second bedroom/closet and gave a looksee. Since a bitch was kid free, I used my second room for clubbin' clothes. And don't be all up in my Kool-Aid wonderin' how I gots a two bedroom with no kids, dat shits confidential. I will say that pussy does a body good, draw yo own conclusions. I had shit from Rainbow for when hitting up house parties to Oky Coky and Ellesse; a bitch ain't play. And no, I didn't work, but that ain't stop me from gettin' mines; as I said draw yo own conclusions. My cell rang interrupting my search, frowning, I pulled out my cell saw who was callin', smiled and pressed talk. "Hey lover." I purred. "Hey, I wanna see you." A robotic voice said. "Sure, when?" I quickly agreed, 'cause money was calling. "Now, should be a cab waitin' out front. I'll be waitin'." Grabbing my keys, I strode to the door and sure enough a yellow cab sat idling at the curb. Stepping out I locked the door, turned and came face to face with a snarling Kelly. "Hoe you got a lot of nerve putting hands on my momma!" She growled. "Look lil girl, stay in yo lane and get out my damn face. Yo moms knows why I tagged that ass, now if there's a problem, have her come see me." Kelly's lips twisted. "Fuck that, I'm seeing you.." I tagged her wanna be grown ass right in the throat, shutting down all dat rah rah shit she was splitting. Kelly gasped and wheezed, eyes wide in panic 'cause she couldn't get no air, hands clawing at her throat. With a smile I sidestepped her no wind having ass and walked over to the cab; got in and we pulled off. The cab pulled over on South Marshal Street. At one time dis street had been the go to spot for it all; pussy, dick, drugs, guns, you name it all.... all run by my nigga Errol God bless da dead. Now da shit was deader than a hooker with AIDS pussy, ain't nobody fuckin' wit it. Walkin' up to a blue one story complete with wheelchair ramp, I rang the doorbell, heard the motorized wheelchair approaching and pasted on a smile; cause in bizness the custie must be made happy. That way when the payout is due your gonna end up with an incentive bonus, trust, yo girl knew from experience and wouldn't lead you astray. Fuck we're all strugglin', tryin' to make a dollar outta five cents. The door swung open and there stood....well, sat dis trick named Ty, short for Tyrone. He wheeled back a lil allowing me to enter. Tyrone 'Ty' Hamilton used to stand five nine when his legs functioned. He was tar black, not that ashy black neither, but a smooth flawless black. Like he rubbed down every day with coco butter or some shit. His hair used to be worn in long ass corn rows, but was now worn short to his scalp. His eyes were a cute shade of brown that seemed to sparkle. Even though life had sucked the juice outta his legs, his upper body was well developed from years of physical therapy. Walkin' in, I bent down, clasped the chairs arms and gave Ty a kiss. Our tongues dueled for a hot second before I stood and closed, then locked the door. Ty smiled, showing off straight whites, grabbing an electro larynx off his lap. Ty put it to his throat and said, 'Damn yo, you look sexy as fuck Tay'. My dick hard just lookin' at chu." He bit his knuckle and groaned which sounded crazy as fuck. "Well, I'm here and I'm all yours daddy." I sexily whispered, then proceeded down the short hallway and into Ty's bedroom. Clean hardwood floors clicked under my heels as I entered. A queen sized bed perfectly made up, end table, TV and dresser made up Ty's bedroom. Ty wheeled in and I idly wondered if he'd ever gotten some payback against the dude responsible for putting him in that chair. I of course knew who did it, but unless Ty was paying extremely well for that info, I ain't got shit to say. Anyway, dude had shot Ty in the throat, hitting his spinal and vocal cords. Divesting myself of jeans and top, I paraded before Ty in matching dark blue bra and thong set. His eyes followed my progress as I stopped before him and pulled his wifebeater off. He raised himself up far enough to remove his jeans and boxers, which I eagerly did. A thick, tar black nine inches revealed itself hard as a rock with pre-cum dripping from the mushroom shaped head. "Yum." instinctively I licked my lips. "Can I taste?" Ty moistened his lips. "You can do anything you want." His dick jumped in anticipation. With a wink, I kneeled and slowly licked from base to tip, kissed the head, swirled my tongue around the head, opened wide and sucked on only the head. Teased the frenulum, worked up some saliva and gave it to him sloppy wet. Ty moaned and jerked in his chair, his hands tightly clenched the arms. 'Shit, fuck girl." he gasped through his voice box. Reaching behind me, I unhooked my bra releasing 36D cup slightly upturned breasts, then I shimmied out of my thong and smiled. Ty's eyes stretched as he took in a fat, hairless pussy so juicy and delicious it put Georgia peaches to shame; I'm just sayin'. Ty rubbed and squeezed miniscule fluffy cheeks like his ass was kneading dough; I made one cheek bounce. I grabbed both cheeks, parted 'em wide and let him get an eyeful of the luscious center of my Tootsie Pop. Twirling, I straddled the chair, pulled a Durex from off the floor where it fell when I took off my bra. Rolled it on, then slowly slid down on that hard, pulsing rod that filled me up oh so well. Ty groaned, but because his voice box lay under my thigh; I couldn't hear shit. I threw both legs atop his shoulders and started throwing it hard body. My juices covered every inch of those nine inches as I rocked, rolled, and bounced our way to cumming. Ty slid a finger in my ass and with a grunt I came, followed by Ty; who forcibly gripped my hips so hard I know I'd have fingerprints come morning. nothing a lil make up won't hide. Two hours and three fucks later, with two thousand in my pocket, that incentive I told ya'll about; I decided to jump on the bus and made my way through the city. My plan was to do a lil shoppin' at the three stores downtown. I know right. Yes I said three stores, and one of those was a jewelry store. Go figure. Anyhoo, the bus, full of cryin' babies, one who'd taken a dump and was smellin' up the bus, a few old people with them damn push carts you put groceries and shit in blockin' the fuckin' aisle, finally made it downtown. Trust, I pushed and shoved; and when the back doors opened I was the second motha off that bitch. Downtown was crowded with people on lunch breaks, just chillin' and shoppin'. First stop, Chen Jewelers which catered to the hood stars. They all copped their jewelry from Chen's until they hit the big time and advanced up to Kay jewelers and from there it was trips to New York for their pieces. I got me a pair of hoops and some diamond studs, then it was on to Twenty-One and Above clothing store; which sold a good quality of bootleg and more merchandise. Then, since I was near Wendy's, I decided to go inside where I ordered the new Baconater burger and fries; and got diggity damn that shit was delicious! Then back on the bus I went, headed for home to get ready to see me some Shaggy! Nelton Court was busy as usual. Glenda, a few doors down, had her front door open and was loudly playing reggae music. When Shaggy started crooning, 'bout 'It wasn't me.' I started bouncing my shoulders and poppin' my hips to the beat. Oh yeah I'm surely up in there in, I glanced at my watch, four hours. 'Get it Taylor!' Glenda came flying out her door and started whining her hips. 'You going to see Shaggy tonight?' Glenda asked me. 'Sure am, and I take it by the music playing yo ass going too?'

Glenda nodded and we slapped palms. 'How you getting' their Tay?" 'Dove's pickin' me up, why?" I knew her ass wanted to bum a ride. 'I wanted to get a ride, you think she'll mind?" 'If you gassing up her car, I don't see why not." Glenda handed me twenty bucks. 'Don't leave without me." she said. 'I won't, be ready by seven." Turning, I made my way to my apartment, ignorin' Kelly's ass who sat on her stoop with the stink face, her red throat causin' a smile to form. I slowly walked past, givin' her ass nothin' but space and opportunity. Hell, let a bitch I had beef wit' who'd punched me in the throat turn her back on me while walkin' by and I'm on her ass, believe dat shit. All Kelly did was suck teeth, Rosalie sucked the dentist's dick three months and five days out the week for. 'Where's Brick? Oh probably with Toni, like earlier." That's right, I said it and ain't feel bad neither. Kelly glared, rolled her eyes and spat, 'Fuck outta here Taylor. Brick's where he is, mindin' his, which is what you should be doin'. Oops, you don't know how cause you to busy tryin' to be young out here. Besides, my sister would never cross that line." She said in this know it all tone. So I pulled out my cell, scrolled through my pics, leaned in her face and showed Kelly her sister and her man swappin' spit. Yeah, I snapped dat shit. Tol' you I was filing that hot shit away for later. Her eyes got all shiny and shit, then filled with water. Tears streamed down her face before she swiped at her eyes. 'Before you step to dis old bitch, make sure yo own yards trimmed sweetie." I nicely added, turned and strode to my door; thoughts of Kelly no longer a fuckin' factor.

CHAPTER 3

Three and a half hours later, perfection accomplished. I gave the mirror a last look, green and red five inch stiletto tie up the calf heels, showcasing firm shapely calves and thighs; a red halter mini dress, with green thong underneath (a true bitch always matches completely). Giving a nice glimpse of plump cleavage, I turned to the side, bounced a cheek, then continued my perusal. My shoulder length black hair with blonde tips was in spiral curls and I wore minimum jewelry just some earrings; cause if shit broke out and I had to fight or flee, no way was I loosing jewelry in the process. Picking up my purse, my cell rang 'Hello." I answered, 'C'mon girl I'm outside." said Dove. Hanging up I opened the door, stepped out, locked it, turned and almost knocked Glenda's ass over. "The fuck!" I snapped. 'Sorry, I was getting ready to knock." Glenda quickly explained cause her ass knows the ghetto switch flicks on and off real fast; and her punk ass, who can't fight her way out a paper bag, ain't want it with me. 'Hmm." I quickly gave Glenda's ass the once over, cause ole girl couldn't dress to save herself. One time her ass came outside wearing purple and green pinstriped leggings and an orange flowered shirt! Tonight Glenda wore black jeans, pink Reeboks and a red tee with an old pic of Shaggy from his 'Boombastic' days on the front, while her hair was done up in twists. Passable. 'Really, I'm sorry Taylor." With a stern look, I could feel the ghetto switch itchin' to turn on. Dove beeped the horn, saving her ass from a beat down. 'Let's go ya'll damn! I gotta find parkin'!' Shouted Dove. Turning, Glenda scurried towards the car, then jumped in the backseat. With a mean strut I followed, feeling great from the eyes of Nelton Courts occupants watching and wishing they were goin'. The Bushnell was packed with people. Car horns blew in disgust from traffic moving at a snail's pace. 'See, ya'll bitches so busy tryin' to look cute, now I gotta hunt for a space." griped Dove as her neck craned lookin' for a parking space. "There go one!" Glenda yelled, pointing at a side street where an available space sat between a grey Honda and a black Impala. It took Dove's ass two tries to get into it, on the third she managed to lightly tap the Honda's bumper. 'Ooo!' Glenda screamed, like Dove caused a hit and run. 'Girl shut da hell up!" we both stressed than exited the car. 'If you gonna hang with us," snapped Dove, 'then you need to not be all loud and shit unless called for cause we don't do scary, lame hoes." 'Sorry, sorry." reiterated Glenda as we walked towards the Bushnell. Streams of people, coupled up and alone, headed for the Bushnell while vendors sold hotdogs, sodas and more. One dude who leaned against the wall claimed to be selling Shaggy tickets for sixty bucks. I snorted, looked his bummy ass up and down and kept it pushin'; cause any sane person knew if your sellin' you'd double, not lower the price. Shit, his ass was probably sellin' some fake shit he'd printed up or were from an old show. Glenda's dumb ass actually stopped to see if the tickets he was selling were seated better than what she had. With a tooth suck, Dove walked back, snatched Glenda's arm and yanked her ass. 'Girl, ain't nobody tryin' to babysit yo ass, I left Jeffrey behind alone for a reason." Glenda gaped. 'You left yo son home...alone?" she said not believing she'd heard right. Dove stared at her., 'What? He's sleep and I locked his room door. What's the problem?" Not wanting to get cursed out or worse, for Taylor to go off, Glenda refrained from speaking on what was wrong with everything Dove had said. 'Okay, I got it, I'm ready to get wasted." Dove and I laughed. 'Its turnt up girl. C'mon wit' yo square ass." chided Dove. Glenda smiled and followed behind me as we jumped in the shortest line. Dove pulled out two tickets, gave 'em the once over and stepped up to an older Hispanic chick who took the tickets, barely spared them a glance and waved us through. Once inside, Dove and I hi fived cause those tickets were faker than K. Michelle's ass. Glenda handed over her ticket and quickly caught up with me and Dove; then we headed for our seats, which were on the floor, row G. Had to throw that out there so you'll see a bitch of my caliber don't do balcony. Soon as we took our seats the lights dimmed and everybody started clapping as DJ Smoke from QTQ radio stepped on stage. "Sup Hartford! Ya'll ready to get this party started?!" People cheered, some changed Shaggy's name. "A'ight ya'll Shaggy bought a special guest, welcome to the stage Beres Hammond!" Girl I jumped up and started yellin' like I hit a scratch off ticket. Hell yeah! Beres was my boo, I'd eat his ass with a side of grape jelly. Ump. Beres sang all my favorites and I enjoyed every song. His melodic voice soothed and aroused me at the same damn time. Half an hour later Shaggy's sexy ass came out. Dude was too damn cute to have a f'd up name like Orville, ain't that a popcorn? Ole Orville could still get it though, for real. Dude sang three songs, told us he'd just got married and was cuttin' shit short to start his honeymoon. Is he fuckin' serious?! So what my ticket was fake, I got dolled up to see his ass and this how he plays it?! I wanted to flip the switch and show my natural black ass, but the Bushnell ain't play that shit, cause po-po was all over the place. Frowning and foot tapping, I glared at passing patrons, mentally daring anyone to bump me or step on my foot while making my way outside. 'Girl why you mad, we saw that shit for free," Dove said as we started walking back to her car. 'Free? How'd you manage that? I saw you hand over tickets." questioned Glenda, eyes glazed with curiousity. Dove burst out laughing. 'You have much to learn grasshopper." 'Hunh?" 'Girl never mind." I snapped and yanked open Dove's car door. 'Let's to to Sunset, I need some drinks." Dove nodded, started her car and tapped the Impala so hard her ass cracked a brake light. 'Oh fuck me with a twelve-inch shlong! Let me get outta here, a bitch ain't got license or insurance!" She yelled before pulling out and off with a squeal from bald tires. The Sunset Café was just that, a place where everyone and their momma went once the sun set. The café was small as hell and yet they'd crammed in a pool table right by the men's bathroom, while half the dancefloor was taken up by the homemade DJ booth. The owner, this chick name Jesse, owned Sunset and had her family running it while she sat her fat ass home, scarfing down food. Anyway her two daughters ran the bar, her youngest son the door and her cousin DJ'd. Paying the seven dollar entrance fee I stepped through the door first, letting all haters and possible easy marks get an eye full. Dove then Glenda followed. 'Lincoln's 'Lollipop' played and my head bobbed to the beat. I shimmied up to the bar between a purple shiny suit wearin' mofo with a jheri curl and a heavyset white woman whose fat oozed over the stool. A semi cute, semi cause ain't nobody cuter than moi, light bright bartender strolled up; towel thrown over her shoulder and said, "What'll it be?" I eyed that caterpillar she called an eyebrow, grimaced and ordered a rum punch, dude next to me said, "I got it Ruthie." which was my plan all along. Smiling, I turned to face shiny suit and almost threw up in my mouth. Besides that played out jheri curl and shiny suit he sported, his face was a mass of cyst type bumps that covered from forehead to chin, cheek to jawline. That was bad enough, but then two of dem shits popped and started oozing pus and blood. That was pretty horrible too, but the shit smelled like fresh clotty period blood. Gross! "Thanks sexy." I purred, biting back bile; sipped my drink Ruthie slid my way and quickly looked for an out. Thank God for Dove who walked up and snarled,. "Damn bitch, dis why I don't take yo ass nowhere, cause every time I turn my back yo ass in some nigga face." I put on the puppy dog look, thanked pus face for the drink and quickly made my exit. Sunset was swiftly gathering a crowd which I got lost in until I could no longer feel dudes eyes on me. Dove's ass was in tears she laughed so damn hard. "Fuck you Dove." She wiped her eyes. "It would be a definite improvement. Girl that was a new low for you." she joked. I sipped the last of my rum punch, gave Dove the finger and looked around. "Where's Glenda the good witch?" Dove smirked. "Girl I can't with you okayyy. Anyway I left her ass holdin' a table; you know it's only like eleven of dem joints up in here." "True, well lead the way." Dove turned, bobbed and weaved through the crowd with me on her heels. Mavado played and I started wining in my seat, I peeped Glenda doin' the snake and smirked. Ole girl definitely needed to be brought up to date. Who the hell still did the snake?! Lookin' around I could see buns outnumbered hotdogs three to one, and if those odds didn't change and soon, a bitch was out. Glenda stood. "I'm going to the bar, ya'll want something?" "You treatin'?" Dove and I said, Glenda nodded. "Then hell to the yeah I want a drink." I said. "Me too." replied Dove. "I'll have a sex on the beach." I glanced at Dove's ass and chuckled, cause that drink would be the closest she ever came to havin' her bird like frame sexed on the beach. I'm just sayin'. "I'll have a Long Island iced tea." I ordered, then added, "and light on the ice." "Okay, be right back." "So whatchu think 'bout Glenda?" I asked, wanting to hear Dove's thoughts. She shrugged, "Girl dat one needs a lotta work, is she worth it? Remember what happened last time you 'taught someone'." Dove threw up quotation marks. The ghetto switch jiggled. I know dis hoe ain't tryna do me and in a crowded club at that, where ears hear everything. I arched a brow to let her ass know her dig was received, processed, calculated and a return dig would be served when I felt the time was right. Dove nervously coughed. "I'm just sayin' Taylor why put yo self out there?" Hmm, I silently thought. "How's lil Brian? Does Jeff see his uncle/daddy?" Pow! That tricks jaw damn near hit the table. Brian was her older brothers twin, they shared the same mother, but different daddies cause Dove's ole triflin' ass momma got it poppin' while pregnant. I think I read somewhere the shits called superfecundation bipaternal twins. Anyhoo, Dove claimed her ass was saucy after a night spent partying and ended up fuckin' Brian's ass. Now, I could've swallowed it if Dove hadn't fucked Brian a rack of times, ended up pregnant, kept the baby and was currently passin' his ass off on the next man. Glenda returned, balancing a Corona and our drinks. "Thanks," Dove sullenly muttered. Feeling better, I glanced around while Drake's 'Hotline Bling' played and was pleased to see more hotdogs had arrived. "Wanna dance?" A voice asked, I looked up and saw Sammy waiting on Glenda's response. "Uh, sure." she stammered, wavering smile on her face. Sammy was a nice guy, he installed cable for a living, had no kids and his own apartment; Glenda probably couldn't do any better. I'm just sayin'. Luckily the DJ threw on Trey's 'Slow Motion' like he knew her ass ain't have no damn rhythm. "I'm goin' to the ladies, can you watch my drink?" Pleaded Dove. "Gone girl, I gotchu." I watched Dove disappear in the crowd and barely contained a yawn. Weak hoes that can't stand up for themselves get the verbal smack down or worse. Smirk. Remy Boyz ft. Fetty came on, I hopped up and started dancin'. Before I knew it, dis sexy mofo with some LL lips and an Idris Elba face was getting his grind on behind me. Dove lucky her ass came back when she did, cause ole boy was workin' me right and the last thing on my mind was missin' out cause I'm watchin' a damn half drunk drink, chile please. Turning around I gave dude the full frontal view of alla this, bam! That's right boo, drink it in and try not to drool. Anyhoo, dude stood around five eight and was the color of dark chocolate. Now most dark women like moi, would pass over such a fine specimen, but not Taylor James; I don't discriminate boo. I love all dick, in all flavors; just don't bring no Vienna sausage to the meal, 'cause I'd need like four cans just to do me right gotdamnit! Dudes smellin' good, so I step closer and tally up before wastin' anymore of my time. Hell, my shits valuable feel me. Low haircut minus waves, check, straight teeth, not pearly white, but doable, check, the frame is kinda on the slender side but again doable, then I glance down and this ninja got a fake leg! Aww hell to the no! Taylor Janae James don't want no stub, nub, or stump rubbin' all against this goodness. And why da fuck is he broacastin' dat nasty shit in jean shorts. "Nah boo, I'm good." I snap. "No way yo ass can keep up, you can't walk without help. If yo fuck game like yo leg, I'd throw dat shit out the window and leave." I gave his ass the turn and strut away.

Mad, I pushed my way through the crowd reat to go. I looked around for Dove and or Glenda. Seeing neither, I headed for the restroom. I walked in and gasped. Dove's crazy ass was spread eagle atop the sink, Glenda between her legs feastin' like it was Thanksgiving day! "The fuck!" I yelled, reached behind me and locked the door like their hot pussy asses should have done. Glenda jumped up, mouth all glazed, while Dove fingered her extra hairy box to finish getting off. It's a wonder Glenda didn't cough up a hairball; I'm just sayin'. "Glenda, Glenda, Glenda." I chided. "Get over here and let me see yo skills, You do me right, I might let you hang out with me." Glenda scurried over like a mouse on crack, I knew her ass wanted to fit in and would do anything I told her ass. Needless to say, ole Glenda's tongue worked magic, dat ho finally did something right.

CHAPTER 4

Two weeks later I'm chillin' on my stoop when dis dude name Marcus walked by lookin' oh so delicious wit' his high yellow self. Clearin' my throat, I caught Marcus's eye, winked, then waved him over. My pussy woke from nappin' at the sight of bow legs in basketball shorts; his dick print waved hello and my snatch clawed my panties in response. "Sup Taylor, you out early." "Let me find out you clockin' lil ole me's ritual." Marcus smiled, then drug his eyes down my frame. I was wearin' cootchie cutters, so I knew my camel toe was on full display. Smiling, I stood and invaded his space, Marcus chuckled. "Nah." he said. "I just be seeing you out here every morning is all." "Hmm." Reaching out I ran a nail from neck to navel. "You in a hurry?" I whispered by his ear, then licked the lobe. Marcus groaned and said, "Don't start nothing you can't finish Tay'." then gave my ass a squeeze. "Who says I can't? Let's go inside." Marcus gave a quick look around, nodded and followed me inside. Closing the door, I turned and found Marcus so close I'm surprised we didn't bump heads. He pulled off my tank top releasing full, perky 38D's; nipples on hard and ready to be sucked. "Damn." Marcus uttered, lowered his head, flicked out his tongue, swirled it around, then sucked my nipple in his mouth. My shit was meowing and ready for action when somebody started banging at the damn door. Best believe I ignored that shit cause getting' some pipe was more important; when a voice yelled out for Marcus. "Marcus! Marcus Alonzo McNair, I know you're in there! Open this damn door!" Dude froze like he was stuck in vogue position. "Oh shit!" He whispered. "It's my girl, Okra." Like I gave a shit. Marcus was twenty-two, legal ya heard, which meant it's his dick and he could stuff my pussy if he wanted. "Ignore her ass, she'll bounce." I said while sticking my whole hand inside his boxers, thumb and index immediately getting soaked in pre-cum. The banging got louder, I'm sure drawing a crowd. "Tsk, it ain't even noon and already bitches getting' it fucked up." I snarled, scooped up my shirt from off the floor, pulled it back on and barely paid Marcus a glance when I snatched the door open wide as fuck; making damn sure ole Okra's ass could see her man fumbling with his shirt, but shit the shit was inside out, ha! Arms crossed, foot tapping, Okra shot daggers while eying me and Marcus. "The fuck you doin' in there?!" She yelled, stressin' the latter like my house was full of the heebie jeebies. 'Uh..I..see what had happen was..' Marcus stammered and stuttered. " I asked Marcus if he could unstop my tub," I coyly threw out. 'Fuck you Taylor, 'cause that's what maintenance is for and if that's true why yo shirt on inside out Marcus like you got dressed in a hurry?!" She spat. 'Bring yo ass Marcus, I'll deal with you at home!" Marcus ole scary ass raced out the door, kissed her cheek and muttered, 'Nothing happened." before hurrying off. 'And as for you! Mofos are tired of yo hoe ass trying to creep with their men. I know I'm done and once I drag you out yo shit and beat yo ass you'll think twice." Promised Okra. Now honestly, I could see why Okra's upset. Her ass was big, wide, mushed in and full of dimply cottage cheese. She'd lucked upon a nice lookin' man and didn't wanna lose him. But did I give a rat's ass? Hell to the no. It ain't my fault Marcus is curious 'bout all dis, I mean can you blame him? I'm just speakin' the gospel. 'Girl boo, ain't nobody scared of yo out of shape ass; and if Marcus wants to sample these cookies, I'll give his ass all the milk he can swallow. In the meantime bitch, do sumthin' witcho self. You been wearin' dem hair rollers for weeks; if that shit ain't curled yet, it ain't gonna. And hit up a clothes store boo, Mens Warehouse always gotta sale." I broadcasted. 'And how you know Marcus ass was here any damn way? That trackin' device workin' out well for ya?" My face stung something wicked. I had to touch my face to make sure dis bitch ain't slice my shit. When I realized her ass pimp slapped me I took it to her fuckin' face. "You," punch, "gone," another to her eye, "learn today!" I growled, punching Okra dead in the giblets and down she went throwing hands over her face while balling up. "Kelly! Kelly told me! Please stop Taylor, please!" "Hmp, where's all that tough talk you was just spittin' hunh? Get tha fuck away from my damn door!" I yelled, stepped inside and slammed the door. Third drink in hand, cig burnin' in the ashtray, I ruminated on Okra's earlier statements. Payback was a definite must on Kelly's ass; and if Rosalie and Toni wanted it, they could be served up too. And all that shit about bitches bein' tired of me fuckin' they men was ridiculous, so what I'd slept with like three or four. Okay okay twelve, and almost with Marcus, but that shit doesn't count and anyone says different is full of it. Like I told Okra's ass, if they step to me I'm on it. These hoes ain't neva said a word, but smile in my face. I snorted, I wish a trick would step to me about her man's wandering dick. And who names their kid Okra any fuckin' way?! Her big ass should've been named Pumpkin or Rutabaga. Stupid cunt. My cell rang. Glancing at the screen I saw Omaire calling, my anger instantly dissipated, replaced by a wide smile. Omaire was this dude I met on the late night on one of my sweet tooth runs. Omaire had dough, his father was Kidd a rapper who made it big back in the eighties.

Omaire thought that shit was hereditary, but I'm here to tell ya'll it ain't. Omaire can't rap, sing or come up with a good pick up line to save his soul, why you ask? I answered, "Hey boo," "S-s-sup T-T-Taylor, I wanna s-s-see you m-ma." and there you have it. Dressed to impress in a pink, sheer baby doll nightie and kitten heels, I pulled on my trench coat, grabbed my overnight bag and headed out the door where a beautiful, dark purple, fully loaded Maybach 62 awaited. Complete with driver who stood at the ready, who assisted me with my bag, then opened my door. "Thank you Jarvis." I purred. His portly belly jiggled and his cheeks flushed. "My pleasure ma'am." Mann, that Maybach was a beautiful car. It felt like I floated on clouds, tinted windows kept the lookie lou's wonderin' who rode through the hood in such a luxurious car; while others thought about catching it at the light and taking it. Pushing a button, drinks, ice and glasses slid out a panel. "I could get used to this shit." I whispered, not wanting Jarvis to hear and think I wasn't used to nice shit. We jumped on the highway, I poured myself a drink and settled in for the ride. Jarvis pulled up to a beautiful mini mansion out in Concord New Hampshire, where homes started at a milli and change. Jarvis typed in a number on his cell, which changed daily, and the huge ass gate with letter O engraved in the center slowly swung open. Jarvis drove up a winding drive full of picturesque mango, apple and orange trees. Roses, tulips and more dotted the green landscape as he pulled up into a circular drive, placed the car in park, hopped out, grabbed my bag, then opened the door. "Thanks Jarvis." "Have a good day ma'am." he responded. "Oh, I plan on it." Taking my bag, Amid the butler who stood at the doors, protests. I stepped inside, amazement dotting my face, even though I'd seen it all before. Solarium, tennis court, greenhouse and heated pool made up some of the amenities. Omaire had shown me around twice and after seeing the wine cellar and sauna, my ass was tired. Omaire had cheesed and bragged that there was much more to see. I ignored all that and headed to his bedroom. If I ain't movin' in who gives a shit, I'm just sayin'. Anyhoo, there were two winding staircases; one of which Omaire was walking down looking spectacular in grey John Varvatos slacks and a cream colored John Varvatos button up shirt. His reddish colored hair was braided to the back in five zig zagged cornrows, the ends covered in two beads, one white, the other grey. Omaire stood around six feet even with cafe au lait colored skin and chinky ass eyes, full lips, pearly whites and a cleft chin made up quite a nice package. It also didn't hurt that he wielded eight and a half thick inches and knew how to brandish it. "Welcome Taylor, p-please l-l-leave your bag. J-Janice w-will bring it up-upstairs." With a nod, I let my bag drop, gave a wink and met Omaire at the bottom of the stairs; his scent of Giorgio teasing my nostrils. Lips met, tongues sinuously danced, Omaire's hands eagerly cupped, then squeezed my ass causing a moan to slide free. 'Damn m-m-ma, you g-get sexier ev-everytime I s-s-see you." He stuttered. Omaire tasted, smelt, felt and looked like money and my pussy was soaked at the thought of greenbacks and dick. Now if only we could eat and fuck with no conversation, shit would be good; cause all that st-stutterin' was fuckin' annoyin' and made my temples throb. As if readin' my mind, Omaire led me past a few rooms and into the kitchen where we always ate. I mean why sit at a table that seats twenty and it's only the two of us. Anyhoo, the table, big enough for five, held grilled chicken cutlets with Middle Eastern spice rub and baby greens, stir fry veggies in garlic oyster sauce and for dessert chocolate moo cake; which I couldn't wait to sink my teeth into. Talk between us flowed as easy as it could for someone who stuttered with every other spoken word. So believe me when I tell ya'll I was happier than a gay boy with a bag of dicks once we advanced upstairs. A king sized canopy on a raised dais, dark blue thick shag carpet had my heels sinking, armoire and two huge walk in closets. Omaire pulled off his shirt and wifebeater, muscles came into view and my mouth watered at the sight. Yum! Untying my coat, I let it fall around my feet and inwardly smiled when Omaire's eyes bucked. 'D-damn, I t-though that was a-a dress." Walkin' up I placed a finger against his lips to shut his ass up; then kneeled, unbuckled, unzipped and dove inside his boxers as his pants slid to his ankles. Hard, hot, pulsating man meat meet tonsils, slurp! I relaxed my throat and gobbled him down until pubic hairs teased my nose. Givin' good head is a muthafuckin' art. If done right you'll get off as well, trust ya girl always does the dick right! Pussy soakin' inner thighs, I went in for the kill; tongue slowly lickin' the frenulum onto the coronal had his ass squirming in delight. Back up to the slit, probing it with my tongue, down to his balls; lick, suck, a hum. Feeling Omaire squirm, I knew a cum soaked dessert was on the way. Nipples hard at the thought, I tweaked and tugged; traveled downstairs, shoved a finger up my twat and stroked. Three of 'em had me flyin' over the edge just as dessert flooded my mouth. Gulping it down, I smacked my lips, taste like chicken. Syke! But why do we say that dumb shit; cause everything does not taste like fuckin' barnyard pimpin'.

"W-whew girl!" Stuttered Omaire breathing erratic. Givin' his ass a shove, he tumbled on the bed and I jumped on his ass putting pussy dead on dem lips and stutterin' ass tongue.

CHAPTER 5

"**G**url is you still in yo feelings?" I asked Dove's ass, cause I ain't heard from her ass since I interrupted her hairy snatch from bein' smacked on. Hmp, don't be mad cause my pussy looks, smells, tastes and feels better than that eighteen-wheeler wide load she calls a pussy, I'm just sayin'. Dove made this teeth grindin' noise I know she did when she wanted to say somethin', but wouldn't. Weak bitches I tell ya. 'Naw, I'm good. What's sup?" 'Nuttin' chillin'. Callin' to see what yo ass is doin'?" "Well I was actually comin' yo way, Glenda called. She got her rebate check from CRT from when that boiler blew and ruined her Rent A Centa furniture." I smiled. "What time you comin'?" I asked. 'Shit I don't know, Bernard has the car. Plus, I'm tryina find Sheila so she can watch Jeff's ass for me." "Oh, well text me when you get here, maybe I'll go with you." Dove agreed and hung up. I quickly gave what I had on the once over, a form fitting blue jean button up mini dress and strap up the calf wedges. I'd pulled my hair back in a messy ponytail, grabbed my keys and headed out the door. Outside the weather was a balmy eighty degrees with a slight breeze. The usual kids ran around all loud and shit; someone had bought a kiddie pool and filled it with water. Gettin' closer, I could see Rosalie's ass in it, sitting Indian style. The fuck? Her ass ain't even have no grandkids, ole cheap bitch! Without a word I sauntered past, ignorin' her pitiful attempt at startin' a convo with me. A lip curl's all her ass got, until I took it to her wanna be grown ass daughter. Then and only then could her useless beggin' ass say shit to me. Glenda's door was open, the screen unlocked. Ty Dolla Sign's 'Or Nah' played at a comfortable level, the smell of fish (at least I hope it was and not her pussy, I'm just sayin') scentin' the air. 'Glenda!" I called while walking in her shit. 'In the kitchen!" She yelled back. I eyed her furniture, a cream cloth covered couch, a black recliner, two end tables and thought, 'Her shit wasn't destroyed how the fuck did her ass scam CRT? And how can I be down?" Walking into the kitchen I peeped the table laden with macaroni salad, potato salad, a sweet potato pie and fried okra. 'Damn girl," I greeted. 'What's the occasion?" Glenda jumped like I'd shot her in the ass with a BB gun. Uh, hello! Did her ass not respond when I yelled her damn name? Ole dramatic hoe. 'You okay?"

Glenda patted her chest. 'Yeah, yeah. Anyway, how you doing Taylor?" I watched her ass nervously turn the same piece of fish twice before setting down the spatula. 'I'm good, just stopped by to see what's up with you. I haven't seen you since the club." Glenda flushed, swallowed, grabbed the spatula and started removing pieces of porgies and whiting's from the grease. 'Oh, just been busy is all. Whatchu been up to?" I eyed her ass for a hot second. 'Doin' what?" 'Hunh?" 'You heard me. I heard you got a check from the rental office, how'd that happen?" Glenda nervously looked around like it was more than me and her ass standing there. 'Uh....well, see," 'Girl spit it out all damn ready!" I loudly spat. 'I fucked Rich, he authorized the check." My eyebrow rose, eww, Glenda fucked Rich's five hundred pound, one eye roaming, smellin' like Munster cheese ass, gross! Then again, if that fat bastard was doling out checks I'd clamp a clothespin on my nose and ride his fat ass into the sunset! I'm just sayin. 'Really." I drawled out, wheels turning. Glenda nodded. 'Yep, he likes to trick girl and the moneys nice; so I said fuck it." I nodded and took a seat, picked up a piece of porgie and took a bite; the shit was good, not fried to hard not too salty. Glenda removed the fish, set four more in the frying pan, then took a seat across from me, smiling wide. 'I feel you, I feel you. So whatchu doin' later?" I asked to see if she'd keep shit real about Dove comin' thru to hang out. 'Nothin' much." my lips twisted. "Hmm, then why yo ass cookin' all dis food? If it ain't nonma den say dat hot shit, cause I can't stand scary bitches." Glenda took a deep breath. "Oh, I just invited a few people over." I snorted. "And yet lil ole me didn't get one, why's that?" Confusion colored Glenda's face. "I told Dove to let you know." "Word?" I gave a nod. "Maybe she forgot." I lied, then grabbed a bowl and helped myself to Glenda's macaroni salad. "Too much mayo." I thought while wonderin' how to deal with Dove's ass. "I'll be back, gonna run to the store. Need anythin'?" Glenda eyed me up and down, licked her lips and huskily replied. "You. I can't get you off my mind, my tongue." "Ehh, join the club bitch." I started to tell her ass. "Can you promise you'll come back, I'm fiening to taste you again?" I nodded, turned and left her apartment. Why do bitches keep trying me? I'm a good person to have in your corner. I don't start drama, although I'll finish it and yet hoes keep tryin' me. Hell, Rich's ass had enough fat to go around so that everyone could get a turn on the ride while makin' some dough, but I see bitches wanna act shiesty and keep all the treats for themselves. Not! I'm 'bout to put a stop to Dove's bullshit, once and for all. Dove wiped bitter cum from her lips, then looked up between fatty thighs and awaited Rich's orders. The heavy breaths that escaped let her know she'd done her job pleasing him. Rich wiped the sweat off his brow. "Whew! Gotdamn girl, where'd you learn to suck a dick?" Dove leaned in and begin softly kissing the head, she wanted that check, no way Glenda's ass would out do her. 'My brother." Rich momentarily stiffened as if unsure he'd heard correctly, deciding Dove was joking he smiled. 'Give big daddy some of that sweet pussy." Dove hopped up, yanked up her dress and since she wore no panties, the pussy was easily accessible. Rich tightly squeezed her waist just as pussy hairs touched dick head. 'Hold up Dove, no glove, no love. I don't know where yo hairy box been." Ordered Rich, eyes narrowed. 'Sure, sure, no problem." replied Dove. Even though she had a case of crabs, she still felt some type of way when asked to wear a condom. 'Cause dude who'd shared it, like he was sharing a side of fries, hadn't bothered to wear one or to inform; so any chance she got to infect others was a bonus. Opening the Trojan sitting atop Rich's desk, Dove tore it open, rolled it on; then slowly sat down, squeezing her muscles along the way. Rich gripped her ass and started pounding. The swivel chair they sat in slightly rolled on its wheels, making a squeaking noise with every thrust. Dove's mouth dropped as Rich dug all up in her guts; her insides moistened, allowing easier access. It wasn't like she didn't get around, it was more Rich's dick was wide as a mini Billy club and momentarily had her feeling like she was once again giving birth. 'Sss." hissed Dove, enjoying the pleasurable pain. 'Fuck." rasped Rich, then bust a fat one. Feeling extra wet, Dove hopped up and stared at a ripped condom covering the base of Rich's dick. 'Gotdamn it Rich, tha cheap ass condom broke!" She yelled, pretending to be upset while inside she laughed and did the Quan. 'Fuck Dove, you did that shit on purpose!" 'Me! How'd I do that?" Rich gave the stink eye. 'How? How! By squeezing my damn dick that's how! I'm tellin' you now Dove if yo ass gave me anything now's the time to come clean; cause if I give it to my wife I'll kill yo trickin' ass." He calmly stated, pulled off the torn Trojan with a look of disgust and tossed it in the trash. With a smirk, Dove grabbed a few napkins from the stack atop his desk, wiped her pussy, its juices pronouncing the Popeye's emblem emblazon on it; tossed it in Rich's lap, grabbed her purse and replied, 'Nigga I can say the same shit 'bout yo ole fuck anythin' with a pussy havin' ass. Now cut my shit so I can be out, I've got shit to do." Rich frowned. 'Yeah, to go suck a bag of dicks." he harshly muttered. Dove bit her tongue to keep from going off on his ass but once she got hers, he'd soon get his too.

CHAPTER 6

$ 1500 dollars richer, but pissed her check was nowhere near the amount Rich had shelled out on Glenda's ass. Plus, the fact that when she'd hit up Bernard asking when he'd be back cause she needed her car, only to be cursed out and hung up on, she'd been forced to jump on the city bus; something she hadn't done in years. Grabbing a seat, only to grimace when some chick with three kids sat beside her, squeezing the eldest about five between them; while the other two sat on her lap and three diaper bags hit the floor. One that felt like it was full of Similac caught her pinky toe. The youngest had lost his bobo and was screaming like it was the worlds end, while their mother loudly chatted on her Trac phone about some dude name Larry passin' the Bird around on purpose. Pissed, Dove inhaled feet, musty ass underarms, ass, some chicks meaty pussy, cigs and weed; she felt her head pound. Thanking the merciful bus stop Gods that she was only going halfway down the street before getting off, cause she was ready to as Taylor would say, 'flip the ghetto switch'. Reaching up, Dove rang the bell and couldn't contain an eye roll when the chick started yapping shit to her friend on the phone cause she and her ragamuffins had to move so she could get out the seat. 'Winsome, girl I'm 'bout to snap, crackle and pop. Girl, tell me why dis chick hops on tha bus not even for three minutes and now I gotta move Hennessey, Rose' and Peanut, when her think she's cute ass could've walked!" She loudly issued. 'Fuck you hoe! Nobody tol' yo three ghetto baby, four different baby daddy havin' ass to get on the bus with all yo shit and not sit in a seat by yo damn self!" Dove yelled back, then purposely stepped on a Save-A-Lot grocery bag, feeling bread squish under her Nike. She victoriously smiled, 'Now move tramp, get out the way!" 'Hol' on Winsome! Naw girl, if I go to jail call Mannie and nem to come pick up the kids!" People started chanting, 'fight, fight!' while the harried white female bus driver yelled to let Dove pass so she could continue her route or she'd be forced to call the law. 'Bitch!" The chick yelled, damn near tossin' her kids in the aisle she stood so fast. 'Call 'em, and hopefully they'll get here fast enough to save yo ass; cause I'ma beat you down for callin' 'em!" And with that she swung, catching Dove with a powerful blow to the chin. Dove's head smacked into the window, causin' momentary stars and stripes for vision. Windmilling, Dove caught her left cheek with her nails, drawing blood. "Bitch!" They both yelled as the crowds shouts to see some skin intensified. Peanut wandered to the back of the bus, picked up a sticky lollipop someone had dropped and started eating it, while Hennessey grabbed his mother's phone, hung up on Winsome's yelling, 'kill that hoe' and dialed nine one one. Rose wandered to the open doors and almost fell out if a teenaged boy hadn't grabbed him. Dove swung a wild left catching the girl off guard, she tumbled to the floor, hittin' her head on the metal safety clamps to hold wheelchair riders in place and was knocked out cold. Grabbing her purse, Dove scrambled down the bus stairs and took off running. The get together was in full swing by the time Dove made it to Nelton Court. Nervous, Dove kept looking over her shoulder for flashing lights and sirens until she stepped inside Glenda's and felt her jaw drop. Naked bodies swirled and twined around each other on every available surface, others sat in the kitchen eating and smoking. "Watch it." grumbled this dude called Crazy B, as he came through the door carrying two cases of beer with three scantily dressed girls behind him; liquor bottles in hand. 'That bitch was supposed to wait until I got here. I betchu she ain't even charge like I told her ass." Dove muttered, eyes searching for Glenda's stick like frame. Her eyes widened at seeing Rosalie taking it roughly up the ass while giving Jimmy brain. It seemed everyone in attendance had forgotten their significant others.

Dove hoped Glenda had at least remembered to activate the video recorder, 'cause there were a lot of faces she could blackmail later on. Like Wilbur Baxter who was running for city councilman, currently slobbing on Jeremy's dick; or Sara Williams, the mayor's secretary who sat in the corner shooting up. 'Here girl, you look like you could use this." greeted Okra who stood before her in a bikini top that was a size to small, so her milk jugs were smooshed together and spilling over the top; and a pair of pump ums that showcased her funny shaped dimpled ass. Glazed eyes leered causing a shiver to run down Dove's spine. 'Uh..thanks Okra. I..I didn't know you got down with these type parties. What about Marcus?" Dove accepted the clear plastic cup, went to take a sip and halted inches away from ingesting a little pill that sat dissolving on the bottom. Pretending to take a sip, she watched Okra smile and lick her lips. 'Girl, bump Marcus after the way he played me. His ass in the doghouse til I say he can come out. This is a treat for myself, its somethin' I always wanted to try, so here I am." Dove nodded. 'Oh, well good luck with that. Where's Glenda?" Okra gave a sneaky smile. 'She's busy upstairs." she slid closer, the smell of pussy on her breath. 'No need to disturb them, we can have our own party." Wink, wink. 'Drink up boo, then come find me. I'll be waitin'." Turning, Okra walked into the kitchen and swiped a chicken leg, then attacked it like she hadn't eaten in days.

Shaking her head, Dove headed upstairs to see what the hell was goin' on and why Glenda's ass wasn't stickin' to the script. At the top of the stairs was the bathroom and to the left two bedrooms. The bathroom door was ajar, so Dove pushed it the rest of the way and saw Omar snackin' on Toni's pussy. Her ass in the sink, legs splayed wide, her sister Kelly on her knees alternating between tossing his salad and trying to deep throat dick and balls, only to gag upon Omar's thrusting. Her pussy tingled at the way Omar threw the dick, making a mental note to get with his ass before nights end. Just as she made to leave, the shower curtain moved. Walking in further, Dove yanked back the curtain and gasped. 'Bernard! Fuck are you doin'?!" She screamed in outrage. Yeah, she knew what he was doin' hell, everyone knew what he was doin', but he wasn't supposed to be doin' it unless with her. Bernard stood butt naked except for a pair of Beef & Broccoli timbs, his nine inche dick coated in cream as he pounded Aisha from the back. Her hands tightly gripped her ankles as their skin slapped and shrieks of pleasure slid from her lips. 'Fuck! Get da fuck outta here wit' dat dumb shit Dove. You fuckin' up a nigga concentration." growled Bernard as he kept stroking. Aisha glanced up and smirked, wound her hips, then started slamming her ass back and forth; Bernard groaned. With a huff she muttered, 'Don't be mad if you see me getting' my back blown out nigga." She yelped in pain when Bernard threw a bar of soap sitting in the dish, cracking her right in the forehead. Someone laughed behind her. Embarrassed Dove hauled ass out the bathroom. Aisha was Bernard's ex, they supposedly had a child together. A daughter whom Bernard refused to claim, as his seeds didn't produce bitches, only warriors. Every time she ran into Aisha she'd say slick shit about her and Bernard and the good dick he'd put on her. Now after seeing it with her own eyes, Dove knew Aisha hadn't been just talking. Angry, Dove stomped to the bedroom door and flung it open, four couples sexed atop a twin sized bed making it look like a queen as no one hit the floor. The smell of sex was loud, there moans even louder. Dove hit the light to get a better look at the beds occupants. Maria, Lance, Jayshon and Tiffany all were nineteen. Maria's fast ass had just turned sixteen, not caring that big trouble loomed if the police caught an underage girl at an orgy party. Dove turned and headed for the other bedroom. Glenda's son Marvin Jr was eight and spent summers with her, so they planned on three more parties before Marvin Jr came for the summer. Opening the door she found Glenda ass up being fucked by a big, bald, muscular dude her face between firm chocolate thighs. "I know that ain't," muttered Dove sidling closer, breathing erratic; the sounds of Usher drowning out her pounding heart. It was. Fuckin' Taylor laid, smiling wide, glancing up at a stunned Dove. "Mmm eat dat pussy Glenda, damn girl." I moaned, makin' sure Dove heard my every word while inside I applauded, bam! How you like me now hoe! Tears actually flooded her eyes which didn't move me one bit, cause sympathies for the weak, the slow. Dove gave a slight nod, backed away, turned and made an exit. Four hours later the party was winding down when I let a surprise guest in Glenda's back door. She and Dove were holed up in the second bedroom not that either had shit to say to me about it any damn way. A dimple flashed, along with a mouthful of platinum, his canines held two fangs one with a diamond chip, piercing shiny black eyes that saw shit you didn't want them to; and a head full of three sixty degree waves. Curve cologne teased my nose, wakin' up nipples and pussy. 'Hey boo, glad you made it." Brick winked. 'Sheeit, what nigga wouldn't when they hear orgy and party in the same sentence?" Replied Brick. I stepped closer, stood on tiptoes, as Brick stood five eleven and a half and whispered, 'You got my pussy wet as fuck. I wanna swallow yo seeds and ride it til yo toes curl, can you help me with that?" Brick's eyes lowered. 'Hell yeah." 'Good." grabbing his hand, I led Brick into the living room, I'd kicked everyone out once Dove went up and never came back down. I also lied and told Toni and Kelly Glenda needed a store run for round two of the orgy party. Hearing an opportunity to get another round of dick, I could see the apprehensiveness in Toni's eyes disappear before agreeing. I pushed Brick on the couch, pulled his shirt off and my mouth watered. Mother Mary, may I touch and be satisfied by the muscular six pack carryin' man before me, amen. Brick pulled jeans and boxers down to his ankles. I leaned over and inhaled dick and balls, which smelled oh so good. Opening wide I teased his flaccid joint which immediately hardened, so I took him all the way down, making sure that dick was Billy club hard and climbed aboard. Nine thick inches had a bitch happy as hell, Brick knew what he was doin'. Oohh I felt that shit all in my back it was so good. Bouncing, I heard Toni and Kelly's voices at the door and kicked it up a notch; throwing both legs up on the couch's back. I pulled Brick's head down so that he could tend to dese nipples. The door opened and both girls giggled, then halted. I could feel their eyes on me and smirked. "Yes Brick, fuck me!" I yelled loud enough to be heard. "Brick? Did she say Brick!?" Yelled Toni. Kelly turned to her sister. "And why yo ass so concerned 'bout my damn man!" She screeched eyes wide, hands on hips. Toni snorted. "Don't even try it, ain't nobody studyin' Brick's ass." she retorted. Since they were so consumed with each other, I kept stroking. Brick's ass was in the zone; if he heard his girl he ignored her ass, to intent on getting' that nut. "Brick, what the hell's goin' on!" "Finally." I thought. Brick grunted shootin' a bucket of babies inside me. I'd already got mines, so withholdin' the glee I felt, I slowly climbed off the dick. Surprisingly, Brick just sat there makin' no attempt to fix his clothes or to explain what they'd walked in on. Kelly rushed over and started screamin' in Brick's face, while her punk ass sister just stood glarin' at me. With a yawn I stood, ready to go home, shower and maybe hit up the club; when Glenda and Dove came down the stairs. "What the hell's goin' on down here!" Spat Dove, hands on the bathrobe that covered her hips. "Bitch sit down somewhere. Am I talkin' to you? No! Am I in your place? No!" Yelled Kelly. "Bitch? Yo ass da bitch! Wasn't you and yo ho ass sister upstairs in the bathroom givin' it up to Omar a while ago?" Glenda quickly said feeling courageous with Dove and I standing there. Too bad, if shit broke out I'd stand there and watch unless that bullshit came my way. I tell ya, bitches always startin' shit. "I'm out ya'll." "Uh, uh hoe. Yo ass needs to explain why yo ass was ridin' my sister's man's dick!" "Really? She really wanted to take it there? Okay then, let's go there." "This from the girl whose also fuckin' her sisters man?" I scoffed. "Do I need to show and tell, cause all dis jibber jabberin' bullshit is wastin' my damn club time." Yeah, the ghetto switch is all the way on. So once again I grabbed my cell, all while Ms. Motor Mouth tried to back pedal and get her sister to leave. Yeah, they can bounce, once I shut 'em down and send 'em home beefin' and cryin'. I turned the speaker on, walked up on Kelly and shoved the phone all in her face; wasn't gone be none of dat she didn't see it crap. Brick and Toni came into view inside his cars backseat. At first, all you could hear was them flirtin' back and forth, then Toni started bashin' her sister. Then she stripped and an ass shot came into view as she settled atop Brick's lap and started bouncin' all while spewing venom on her sister. "You lying bitch!" Kelly screamed, reached out and punched Toni dead in the face. They started scrapping, Brick who'd sat silently, finally stood, pulled up his jeans and with a cocky smirk on his face from girls fightin' over him; and walked out the door. Again I started for the door, only to be stopped by Glenda grabbing my hand. "Wait, I thought we had plans." I snorted then rolled my eyes. "Looks like you've got your own plans; besides three's a crowd." "What plans!?" Snapped Dove, head and eyes swivelin' between Glenda and I and Toni and Kelly. "Glenda and I have an understanding, an agreement if you will. You know, like the one you set up earlier with Glenda? You remember right? It's the one where you don't invite me to the party. the one where you go behind Glenda's back and fuck Rich for dough. The one where you planned on takin' all the charge at the door money. Need I go on?" Stunned, Dove stared at me, mouth wide. "Don't look so surprised, you seemed to forget who taught yo ass a lil bit of the game you're tryina play; play and fail I might add." "Uh..I..I don't know what your talkin' about girl. Dat dick you was just served done scrambled yo brain." "Naw bitch, my cousin's brain workin' just fine." said China as she entered the house stopping all movement; even the fight between Toni and Kelly. Dove gasped, China was the girl from the bus, a bandage covered part of the back of her scalp. Three kids trudged in behind her, each carrying Happy Meals. "Yeah bitch, small world hunh?!" Spat China who then jumped dead on Dove's ass. The first punch knocked Dove over the coffee table, followed by kicks to leg, hip, stomach and chest. Toni and Kelly screamed out, "Damn!" But made no attempt to stop the fight. "You stupid cunt!" Yelled Dove who caught China's foot on a downward stomp, used all her strength and flung China; who flew back and crashed through the coffee table. "Oh shit!" Kelly yelled hyped about the fight until a side punch to her jaw dropped her ass. Toni dusted her hands, gave me a glare like she'd advanced to the big leagues and wanted to romp wit' me. Smiling, I waited to see how the young tramp wanted to play it. With a tooth suck and middle finger, Toni made her exit.

CHAPTER 7

La Mirage nightclub was enveloped with people. Saucy after six rum punches, I gazed at the dancefloor through the bars mirror; just chillaxin' not particularly lookin' fo' da dick while the concept of what took place earlier swept in and out my mind. After China went through the table and Kelly lay nappin' on da floor, Glenda grabbed her cordless and dialed the law. That was the bat signal to raise tha hell on and that's just what da fuck I did. I swear bitches love to start shit, I'm just sayin'. Like really though, how bout chu get yo life and chill wit' all the b.s., cause da shit is really un-fuckin'-necessary. Drink on E, I flagged down a cute for a white guy bartender with a black and blonde Mohawk and beautiful ocean blue eyes. My first thought was, 'Fuck he doin' in the hood? Didn't his white ass know venturin' on the north end was hazardous to his health no matter the time of day?" My second was, 'Is it true that white boys weren't packin' so they'd eat da hell outta some ass and pussy?" My asshole puckered; hmm, so many decisions. Should I chill or take his ole lookin' like Clay Matthews ass for a spin in the stockroom? "What can I get for you?" "The hell!" Dude stood around six two and had a nice frame and features, but sounded like he'd sucked down a dozen helium filled balloons. Stunned, it took me a second to process what he'd said. I heard 'Can I suck yo pussy?' I swear! Smirk. "I'll have a glass of fellatio....I mean another rum punch..unless you down?" I wiggled my brows, then wrapped my lips slowly around the straw, swallowed damn near the whole thing; snaked my tongue out and flicked the cherry sitting at the bottom of the empty glass. Dude turned bright pink, coughed and knocked over a glass of beer he'd just poured for some ugly, pockmarked faced chick who looked at me all kinds of crazy, 'cause she'd heard my comment. Big eared bitch probably heard what the DJ was thinkin'. Hell, I'm thinkin' to myself and she probably heard that too. Glarin' at her, I dared her ass to say somethin'. I'm like damn, don't be mad boo. If yo ass chose to sit and get drunk in order to serve up the courage to go for yours and I step up and say how you feel and win tha prize. All I can say is 'yo fault' you snooze you lose! "You serious?" he whispered leaning over the bar, breath smellin' of orange flavored Tic Tacs. Ump, I'll Tic his Tac, nick knack paddy whack, give momma yo bone and I'll find my way home; drippin' yo cum behind me, amen! "Hell yeah, I never EVER joke about da dick boo. It's like religion..... you want it, pray for it and bam! It's delivered in all its delicious flavor, ready for da samplin'. He flushed again and I idly wondered was he a damn virgin; cause his ass works in a club for cryin' out loud. Women and some men too have had to approach his ass with similar offers. He looked left, right, then left again, "Okay, okay. Let me get Roxie to cover for me; meet me downstairs by the men's room." He took off, not waitin' to hear my response. "Tsk, sum hoes are so damn thirsty, they give real women a bad name." said big ears. "Now see, dis da shit I be talkin' 'bout. Why dis dog eared bitch so worried about what da fuck I got goin' on? Bitches always wanna take me there, then when I flip the ghetto switch on they ass it's all whoa is me and why me lord. It's you cause yo pussy so dusty you piss powder, dat shit got a cavernous echo when you part yo damn legs." Switch flipped, I evilly eyed her ass from bottom to top, gatherin' the ammo to send her ass on with her tail tucked between her dry ass legs. Cream colored Payless flats, dem corns and bunions had the sides of her shoes oddly shaped, like she'd slid a pear in her damn shoe. Thick ass ankles that were in desperate need of some Crisco, 'cause lotion would laugh it's ass off; knobby knees I knew slammed togetha' when she walked. A knee length maroon skirt that looked like it belonged in church or behind a desk at a doctor's office, with a cream artificial silk long sleeved high necked blouse tucked tightly in, with two lil nubs she called breasts. A few pieces of jewelry dotted fingers and throat, but nothin' to take an ad out about; a pointy ass chin, full lips covered in blood red lipstick, some of which covered her two front rabbit like teeth. A small, thin nose, almond shaped black eyes and a forehead like that artist Sade, which was hella pronounced by that tight ass bun she wore leavin' every (and there were plenty) freckles on display. I wanted to grab a marker and connect the dots to see what I'd come up with; all encased in yellow skin. "I see your problem, your mad cause you light skinned and feel every man in yo Godly presence is supposed to see you and only you; not the pretty, sexy dark bitch next to you. It's ok boo, just realize yo strengths," I eyed her outfit again, "which ain't dat straight laced prim and proper outfit that's chokin' da hell outta yo ass. Recognize when you see greatness and bow da hell down. Shut da fuck up and move along, cause a bitch like me will steal yo man right in yo face, if you had one. I'd fuck him and let him eat dis tasty treat," I patted my snatch. "and send his ass back to you. Oops, no way would he wanna come back to yo fuck only on Wednesdays, missionary ass. So take notes boo and just maybe when da next prospect strolls up to the bar and you've taken yo ass off ya neck, you'll get lucky enough to have dat dried up, ancient vagina of yours lubed up and stretched out." I stood. "Now suck on that, while I go handle mines, like a real woman." I threw back at her mouth gaping like a fish ass and walked off headed for my tryst; and trust, if I missed out 'cause of her, I'd flip the switch on high and chop her ass in the damn throat. Downstairs was full of supplies and furniture as I walked the hall. An arm reached out and grabbed my arm, I swear I wanted to scream like dem white girls who always scream, run and fall. Then kick some balls, reach in my bag, scoop up my straight razor and commence to givin' out a free shave. "Sorry, sorry." he quickly apologized, eyes contrite. Taking a breath to calm racing heart, I nodded and followed him into the shadows. "My name's Brandon by the way and you are?" "Not interested in pleasantries." I told his ass, "I wanna fuck. I wanna buss a fat ass walnut all ova yo dick, than lick it off. Can you handle that?" "Sure, sure. You've got me harder than Chinese arithmetic." I rolled my eyes. "Good, now where we gonna do this?" I snapped, cause who da hell wants to talk about arithmetic, Chinese or otherwise. My pussy's hungry to be filled, stretched and pounded from the front, back and side. Shit, I'd do a handstand if it guaranteed me getting' off, I'm just sayin'. "I've never had a black woman before." lamented Brandon, like dis a confessional. A soft snicker revealed, he'd turned on a small bendable lamp sitting atop a dusty desk. Eyes swiveling, I swiftly took in the room, makin' sure dude ain't have none of his boys waitin' in the wings to pull a train. Not that I ain't up fo' that, but come real with yo shit, don't be tryina take da snacks. On second thought, havin' da pussy beat down to da seams by three or more hard, cum drippin' dicks ain't a bad thang. Anyhoo, cases upon cases of liquor took up the corners; stacked chairs, a few round tables, the desk and a nice sized leather chair made up the room. With a smile I pulled the zipper on my dress, revealing a pink bra and thong set. My dress slithered around my ankles so I struck a pose, then stepped free. "You haven't hunh? Well honey, once you go black you'll be huntin' my ass down cause no other flavor will do." I assuredly stated. Brandon lustfully eyed my goodies, then scurried over like an eager puppy. "Can I touch you?" He reverently whispered, I nodded. Brandon efficiently unhooked my strapless front closure bra, cupped my breasts and hissed, "They're so soft. Is it true what you said about never going back after having sex with a black woman?" A cheeky grin appeared. "You tell me." Reaching out, I undid Brandon's slacks, pushed 'em down and withheld a frown. Black bikini underwear against his skin had the shit lookin' luminescent. Kneeling, I slowly pulled 'em down and smiled, 'aw'ight now,' I silently ruminated. Ole Brandon was eight and a half inches with a thick, juicy mushroomed cap head. Saliva formed, a long slow lick and I was all in; slurp, and voila, now you see it, now you don't. His pubics smelled of Lifebuoy soap as I bobbed, licked and sucked. Brandon whimpered, hissed and inched up on the boat shoes he wore. 'Fuck!" he groaned out. With a quick glance up I saw Brandon's eyes rolling, while his hands fidgeted between rubbing his jaw and stopping inches away from palming my scalp. 'Sss, don't stop. Please don't stop." He pleadingly rambled. 'Oh my lord, that feels so fuckin' good." Now a bitch like me loves praise, so I went all in and gobbled da balls too, then hummed Rihanna's 'Bitch Better Have My Money' which played upstairs. Feelin' his dick swell I eased off with a loud smackin' sound. Brandon's eyes popped open full of lust, desire and the unspoken words of 'Why'd you stop?" Standing, I debated on yankin' my thong to the side, or stepping free, then did the latter. Bounced an asscheek, stuck a finger in my soppin' wet goodies, then let him lick my fingers clean and baby the way he licked, sucked, nibbled and swirled his tongue around dem digits had me ready to spread eagle atop that dusty ass desk. Brandon growled, picked me up and impaled my gushiness to the brim wit' dick. 'Gotdamn!" I yelled loud as fuck, not carin' who heard over the music playin' upstairs. I bounced, rolled my hips and dug my nails in his shoulders, enjoyin' every moment. Who knew white boys had it in 'em! Twenty minutes later I made my way upstairs amid Brandon's annoyin' ass all in my damn ear askin' when could he see me again. Honey chile please, I got what I needed so I'm good.

Unless he's givin' up some duckets, the goods store is closed. As if reading my mind, Brandon quickly pulled out his wallet, rifled through its bills, pulled out seven fifties and handed them over. I in turn rattled off my number and continued to the bar. 'Doris! You want another beer?" shouted that chick Roxie. I smiled at seeing yellow, siddity her ass still sittin' alone at the bar. Walkin' up I slid back in my seat and eyed her ass. 'Damn, you still sittin' here, alone?" I teased. Durin' my absence La Mirage had gotten a bigger crowd. Doris rolled her eyes at me, thanked Roxie and took a sip of beer. 'Don't you need to go brush the hairs out your teeth? I already counted five." I reared back in my seat. 'Aw shit, dis hoe done flipped the ghetto switch to high heat. My eyes narrowed in distaste. 'Listen trick, dat bug up yo twat must've gave you a good ass nut to try and bring it ova here; but you got the right one tonight hoe." I snapped, body hot, eyes fiery, my hands started itchin' a sign that they'd be meetin' her face momentarily. 'I don't give two rats asses 'bout you Doris." I stressed the latter. 'Da dick was good hoe, somethin' yo body knows jack shit about. Dis pussy so good....so creamy, I got a nut and money. Obviously yo ugly ass wants a taste o honey but that'll never happen hoe, 'cause I got somethin' you'll never have, taste." I spat, picked up her beer and tossed that shit dead in her face; and dared her ass to jump bad. Sputtering, eyes wide in agitation, ole Doris jumped from the stool and spat, 'You ghetto hood booger! My outfit costs more than your whole damn ap.." A punch to those flappin' ass lips shut her ass right up. The hoe fell all dramatic and shit; if I wasn't so mad I would've bust out laughin'. Once down, I added a kick stomp that left a nice shoe print on her blouse. 'Learn yo place when you see me hoe." I told her ass. 'As a matter of fact, every time I see yo ugly ass I'ma jump dead in yo shit!" I snapped. I could see security weavin' through the crowd so I twirled, smacked my ass and made an exit.

CHAPTER 8

anging at my door woke me out a good ass dream. Yawning, I lay in bed for a second to see if whoever was knockin' like I owed their ass dough, would wise up and step da hell off; 'cause I was crampin', bloated and not in the damn mood. Rollin' from bed I stretched, dug my boy shorts out my crack and stomped to the door. "Who da hell is it!" I could've looked through the peephole, but chose not to. "It's me gurl. Open the damn door, I gotta pee!" Dove shouted. With an eye roll I swung the door open and eyed Dove who held a paper bag in one hand and a Hot Pots bag in the other. She stepped in, the smell of greens and chicken wafting behind her. Dove passed the bag, bouncing from foot to foot as she raced towards the bathroom. Bag one contained my favorite Paul Mason, a liter of Pepsi and two vanilla Dutches. The Hot Pots bag held collard greens, white rice, two pieces of fried chicken, a slice of white bread and an apple cinnamon muffin. My stomach growled, letting me know my ass was indeed hungry. Dove appeared, wiping her wet hands on the seat of her blue jeans. "So what wind blew yo bony ass ova here? Unless Glenda ain't home so you playin' it off like you really came to see my black ass." Dove stiffened and I knew I'd hit the nail on the head. "Girl you so crazy." "Shit, I wasn't born last night, at night or last year. Her ass needed to practice lying when it came to me, 'cause I saw right through her bony ass. "Hmm." I eyed her, then walked into the kitchen, grabbed two cups and filled both with three ice cubes apiece before stridin' back into the living room where Dove's ass sat conversatin' on her cell. "I don't know." said Dove my ears zoomed in. "Glenda didn't answer....I know....well I'm at Taylor's, you want me to ask her?" "Ask me what? And who da fuck is she givin' my govment to? She knows I don't play that shit?" I thought, ready to toggle the switch and buss her ass in the chops. "Who you on the phone with?" Dove threw up a finger. "Okay, hold on." she took the phone from her ear, then pushed the speaker button on her cell. "Okay boo, go ahead." said Dove, setting down the phone. She dug in the Hot Pots bag and pulled out a Styrofoam container, plastic fork and started grubbin'. "Taylor." "The one and only." I quipped. "It's Rich, I was wondering if you wanted to make a few dollars?" I perked up. "Doin' what and how much?" Rich chuckled. "I ain't say shit funny, but what da hell ever. As long as his ass was speakin' my language, Grant and Franklin, he could laugh himself to a stroke. "A threesome. Glenda's ass is MIA, so I was hoping you'd stand in." "How much?" I repeated. Dove rubbed her fingers together, then mouthed what looked like one thousand, around chewed up chicken. Gross ass. "Fifteen hundred a piece." A grin formed, period cramps be damned! I hadn't started bleeding yet, usually I cramped like hell two days before seeing any blood. Today was day one, not that I hadn't got down before while on the rag, (I'd turn the lights off and keep the blood where it belonged, my business). Dudes would think they'd gotten me all worked up and shit when they were swimming in blood. "Two hours, Dove knows the spot." he answered. "I bet she does." I lowly uttered. "Bet, I'll be ready." "Good looking, and Dove?" Said Rich. "Yeah boo?" "First, stop calling me that shit, I'm not your fucking boo; and second, when you see Glenda's ass let her know I've got something for her." Rich hung up before Dove could respond. "Nice of ya'll hoes to put me down Dove. I'll make sure to remember this lil faux pas." Showered, shaved and cocoa buttered up, I swallowed two Midol, then dressed in a cute black and yellow mini bandage dress with black flat Roman ankle sandals. I pulled my hair back in a loose ponytail, spritzed on White Diamonds, slid on gloss makin' my money makers pop; glanced at my reflection and walked into the living room where Dove awaited, drink in hand. 'Bout damn time, let's be out." The Hilton Hotel sat downtown on the corner of Trumbull Street, made up of separate suites and other amenities like an indoor pool and fitness center. There were quite a few hotels, motels, Holiday Inns; I love that song, where the niggas went to get their fuck on with they're chick on the side. The Hilton was surely the better choice. Dove's cheap ass parked on the street, grabbed her goodie bag and made her exit; swinging the driver's side door open so wide, an approaching car had to swerve to avoid taking her door off. The driver loudly cursed, blared his horn, shot up the middle finger and kept going. 'Fuck yo ole blind, non drivin' ass!" Dove screamed. 'Drivers." she snorted. 'C'mon Tay', dat nigga hates when I'm late." she quickened her stride. The Hilton's doors smoothly slid open, revealing plush furniture, potted plants and cute vases. The scent of apple potpourri coated the air as Dove bypassed the concierge, front desk and headed for a bank of mirrored elevators. An older couple, one holding a teacup Yorkie, waited as we strolled up. Who I assumed was her husband kept leering at me, then finally licked his thin lips. Ugh! Dude was well past my cutoff date with his grey facial hair and saggy neck skin. Yuck! I could picture extra wrinkled balls that hung by kneecaps, grey wire strands of pubic hair. He looked like skin and bones beneath the sweat suit he wore, grey hairs protruded from ears and nostrils. I quickly stepped on the elevator once it arrived because lookin' at his ass was makin' my cramps return. They stepped on smellin' like mothballs and Ben Gay. I swear I heard bones creakin', poppin' and shit, nasty! Dove pushed the button for the tenth floor while the elderly couple selected the ninth. "How are you lovely ladies doing today?" He drawled, his voice twanging with a heavy southern accent. Dove sucked her teeth. "Good. Where ya'll from, cause yo ass countrier dan a mafucka." the old lady gasped and clutched imaginary pearls. "Well I never! You northern women are some rude creatures." She spat, her light blues watery as fuck. "Bitch you and yo walkin' dead ass man need to mind ya'll mothafuckin' b.i., 'cause talkin' to me and mines will get you robbed and beat da fuck down." Dove spat. Luckily for the couple, the elevator arrived on the ninth floor, the doors slid open and they hurried out so fast the wife/girlfriend tripped and almost bussed her face on the floor. Dove burst out laughin' until tears rolled. I stared at this fool, shook my head and followed behind her down the hall to room ten eleven. "Ready?" With a nod, Dove opened the door and stepped inside a room decorated in tones of tan, maroon and cream. Soft jazz music filtered through hidden speakers, two platters sat atop the table, one full of apple slices, oranges and more while the second held cheeses, crackers, dip and celery sticks. "Do you need to shower, or change clothes?" I asked. "Nah." I shook my head. 'I'm good, but feel free to go do you." Dove eyed my ass like she didn't trust me alone with Rich's ass. Shit, I would've been offended if da shit wasn't true. 'Well come keep me company while I change right quick." I followed Dove into a huge heated floor tiled bathroom which boasted heated towel racks, a huge sunken tub that could seat five comfortably, a frosted glass encased shower with dual shower heads that eight could sex in without steppin' on anyone's toes. Two full sinks, one with track lights and two toilets; one with a seat, one without. 'Fuck they need two toilets for? And where's the seat?" I asked as Dove stepped free of jeans revealing a holey pair of blue panties. She snickered. 'Girl dats a bidet, not a toilet." she said like her ass was all knowledgeable and shit. Her ass dropped out in the seventh grade and at twenty- eight had yet to get her damn GED. I'd heard about bidets, but until today I'd never seen one. Turning from the bidet, I gasped at the ragged, dingy bra Dove wore; one of its straps held together by a big, pink safety pin white women used to pin cloth diapers on their offspring. 'Girl dem drawers and bra have gone well past da expiration date." Dove's lips curled up in distaste. 'Whateva hoe, don't act like yo ass don't own several raggedy pairs too." 'Duh, but I'm classy enough to not wear my shit outside the house." An odor like spoiled lunchmeat assaulted my nose hairs. I inhaled and frowned. 'Please tell me why yo ass smellin' like a factory brewin' infectious diseases." Dove's face flushed an unbecoming shade of red. 'Fuck you Taylor, yo ass always got some slick shit to say. Maybe I have a glandular problem, which is why I brought a change of clothes, hoe." She snapped, with a lotta neck and eye rollin'. 'Girl bye. Just hurry up and scrub yo snatch, douche and do whateva need be so I can make dis dough and be out." I replied. 'Oh yeah, I was wonderin' if we could switch shit up." an eyebrow rose. 'Switch shit up how?" I questioned Dove. Now her ass lookin' all around the bathroom and shit, like we ain't been in dis mafucka a good three minutes already. 'Well, instead of me doin' you, we do each other before settin' Rich right." Laughin' I stared at dis dumb hoe in disbelief. 'You serious?" Dove nodded, a tense look replaced with one of eagerness. 'Yeah, I mean I like to get off too, so why not?" 'Uh, how 'bout 'cause you'll fuck anythin' with a third leg? How 'bout 'cause yo ass smells like yo snatch needs CPR and you want me to put my mouth on you? Girl you done lost yo rabbit ass mind, now hurry yo ass up." Three minutes later we stepped out, Dove dressed in a leopard print leotard with zebra print thigh high boots; her hair done in big loose curls, Ump, some bitches will slap anything together, maybe she packed her bag in the dark. I'm just sayin'. Anyhoo, moi strutted out lookin' like da diva I am in a sheer blue cami one piece I'd worn underneath my dress. I ditched the heels, fluffed my hair and bam! Perfection.

Dove knocked twice, then opened the bedroom door, the sounds of Usher floated throughout the room. Rich's fat ass lay naked, dick in hand, smile leeringly wide. "Ah, the entertainment has arrived." Dove swished her nonexistent hips into the room. "Hey baby, sorry for da wait. I had to make sure I looked good for you." she purred. "Yo ass needs to go back and try a lot harder." I thought, watching Dove's performance. Rich barely paid her ass any attention as his eyes were glued on me. "Come on in, let's get this party started with ya'll dancing." As if on cue, Rae Sremmurd's 'Come Get Her' begin to play. Dove rocked her hips while I turned and made my ass clap, then bounce up and down. As I said before, I might not have a lot of junk in the trunk, but I can work it like I've got K. Michelle's ass. "Okay," panted Rich. "Feel on each other and take dem clothes off. I wanna see some skin!" He bellowed, like Rae was rappin' at full volume or some shit. Dove walked over and started rubbin' and caressin' my 38C's, her breathing erratic. Reachin' out I did the same, divestin' her of that horrendous get up she called an outfit, then felt my eyes widen. Now it ain't like I've never seen Dove naked, 'cause I have, plenty of times. It's just every time I see her big ass nipples I was amazed; her joints were so big she could breast feed three at once. They looked like a big ass silver dollar and when she squeezed 'em milk shot out. Come to find out, when she didn't feel like feeding Jeff, she'd stuff a titty in his mouth and breastfeed his ass! That hoe definitely had problems, too many for me to go in on at the moment. My breasts popped free, Dove rubbed her tire sized nipples against mines; I shivered and the bitch moaned. If only she knew that shit wasn't pleasure, but pure unadulterated disgust. Head lowered, Dove latched onto my nipple and started suckin'. All I could think about was her man-child suckin,' chewin, and swallowin' breastmilk, gross! 'Hell yeah, bring dat show over here!" Rich loudly growled. Granting Rich's wish. we took it to the bed. Rich hopped up, seven inches on hard and drippin' pre-cum, to get a better view. Layin' on my back I let Dove go for hers cause like I said earlier, ain't no way in hell am I puttin' lips to dem nipples or her funny smellin' pus'. 'Dis hoe gotta lot of balls.' thought Dove as she kissed a trail down Taylor's body, semi hate heating her veins along the way. Why couldn't her body look like this? Why'd men take one look at her and decide she was only good enough to fuck? Why'd she get stuck with a case of crabs when Taylor got her fuck on just as much, if not more; and yet her ass was disease free and had men clamoring to wife her triflin' ass. I parted my legs, Dove's tongue eagerly licked and I felt my eyes close in pleasure. Ole gurl could eat some punanny okay; had my ass inchin' off the mattress within minutes. Rich climbed abed and tapped my forehead with the head of his dick, leavin' a wet trail of pre-cum behind. 'Suck my dick." he half pleaded, half ordered. I eyed those seven inches and smirked. 'Slide on a condom." Rich frowned. 'Nah, I'm payin' for shit and what I want is my dick sucked." he spat, jelly rolls of flab jiggling with every word. 'I can do it daddy." purred Dove, eagerly scramblin' to her knees to deliver on her words. Rich fell back on the bed so quick and hard, my ass lifted a good two inches. I rolled, squatted and put my pussy dead on his lips, then hissed when his tongue swept out and got a taste of heaven. Once again jealousy reared its head cause her jaws were at work, while princess Taylor got her pussy ate; something Rich refused to do with her. Dove quickly jumped up and on Rich's dick, condom free. Her plan to pass on the crabs Omar's dirty dick ass had given her, then when he fucked Taylor she'd get it too. 'Oooh daddy, you're so big." lied Dove, who barely felt Rich inside her from all the previous dicks that had recently stretched out her walls. Dove bounced and rolled her hips while shootin' daggers at Taylor. For the next two hours Dove did all the work while Taylor was given easy shit. Like Rich had her dance again and he even strapped it up for a romp between her thighs, only to quit and eat her out again. When Rich finally handed over the money, her pussy was dry and sore; and her asshole felt like if she farted her intestines would hit the floor. Back on the elevator, Dove gave an eye roll. 'What's yo problem?" I asked Dove, like I gave a shit. I knew her ass felt some type of way, but did I care? Hell to the no, instead I pulled out the extra $500 Rich had given me, bringin' my total to $1800 compared to the G she made. Dove smacked her lips. "What happened to what we talked about Taylor? I thought you were down, instead I did all the damn work." Dove rubbed her jaw, guess her ass had a flashback, oh well. "I never agreed to anythin' you assumed. You know what they say about assumin' shit don't you?" "Whateva Tay' and don't 'assume' I don't know Rich hit you off with extra cash." she snapped causin' the switch to jiggle and me to laugh. "He sure did. Don't be mad boo, step yo game up. I taught you better." The doors slid open and Dove stomped through the lobby, bumping a few patrons along the way. Back home I called up one of my tricks, asked if he'd rent me a car; he agreed with a sex raincheck. I didn't mind 'cause Aaron was a certified freak when it came to sex. I met Aaron last year at the Jamaican Parade. He was actually over my age limit as he was now twenty six, but for him, I made an exception. A quick change into a jean mini, white Jordan's and a blue and white top, I was out the door and on my way to sex Aaron and pick up my rental. Aaron Jefferson was a cutie for an older dude. Well he wasn't really old, but you get my drift. Aaron had been in the U.S. illegally since eighteen. He wanted me to marry his ass for a green card, but ain't enough money bein' discussed for that shit to happen, I'm just sayin. Aaron's ass hung out on the Avenue at his boy's Jamaican Bakery until dis club called Kabbalah opened at five. That shit would be full of Jamaicans wilin' to music and yes dem mafuckas are crazy, so believe every story you've heard. One time I was chillin' up in Keney Park, Aaron rolls up and starts goin' off cause some dude was in his parkin' space; like parks had assigned parkin' and shit. Anyhoo, they got to arguin' and shit, next thing I know, Aaron reverted to patois, a sign that shit was goin' left quick fast. Dude swung, missed, then screamed in pain, Aaron had stabbed his ass with what looked like a fuckin' machete so damn fast, even I didn't see it. Then everybody started rumblin' until shots rang out. I hauled ass, and didn't see or hear from Aaron's crazy machete wieldin' ass for three months. I saw dude he'd stabbed up in KFC with a shit bag and was grossed the hell out. Anyhoo, I stepped in Pepper's, head bobbin' to sexy ass Bob Marley comin' thru the speakers. The delicious smells of beef patties, curry goat, ackee, saltfish and more scenting the air. 'Ey babe you finally make it 'ere." greeted Aaron followed by a hug and kiss. "Hey Aaron, sup Peppa?" I greeted, walked over to the fridge, grabbed a ginger beer, popped the top and gulped down half, then burped. Pepper laughed. "You a wild gurl sien." I shot up the middle finger. "Where's Janet?" I asked. Janet was Pepper's wife of two years. They'd been together nine and had a three year-old son. She only stood four foot seven, had to weigh a good two thirty, most of it breasts and ass; and was a real sweetheart, unless she felt you wanted her man, then the craziness slid out. 'She in de back makin' de food." I headed for the kitchen where Janet stood at the stove, hips poppin' as she stirred a big ass silver grey pot. The reggae artist Gage playin' from a radio atop the counter. 'Ump, dats why yo ass pregnant." I jokingly stated. Janet turned spoon in hand and smiled. 'Hey Taylor, where you been girl?" Janet smilingly asked. 'Girl you know me. If it ain't a big dick and a pocketful of dough, onto the next one." Janet chuckled. 'Next!" We both yelled out. 'Where's lil Peppa?" Love shone from Janet's eyes at the mention of her son. 'With grandma Pearl. I'll be scooping him later. You should come with, you know Peppa's crazy 'bout chu." And he was, dat lil nigga didn't F with nobody if I was around. If I'm sittin', he's on my lap. If I go to the bathroom, he's cryin' and kickin' til I come out with his cute self. 'Maybe, gotta see if dicks on the menu first." Janet nodded, turned back around and removed pot from flame. 'Hand me those chopped potatoes." Doing as asked, I idly wondered why Janet and Peppa didn't hire help to get shit done faster. 'A'ight Janet, let me get back out here with Aaron's ass." We hugged again before I made my way back to the front. Two young chicks showin' lots of skin stood flirtin' with Peppa and Aaron. 'Cause I ain't a jealous bitch, nor is Aaron my man, I let him do him while I snatched up a coco bread and took a bite; wondering when Janet's 'another bitch around my man' radar would alert. When the door swung open and Janet appeared carryin' a tray laden with bagged jackfruit chips, fried plantains and different breads. 'So Pepper, when we gonna hook up?" Asked chick one. "Cause I've been dying to wrap these lips around your fat cock." Pepper tried to bat signal ole girl who started rubbing on his chest, while Aaron and chick two conversated. I could hear Janet's foot tappin' along with the tray slamming down atop the counter. Pepper made a move, but chick one followed, smacked his ass and whistled; which quickly ended in a shriek. Janet had come from behind the counter, grabbed a handful of her hair and gave a forceful yank. 'Bitch, fuck is yo problem! Pepper get this fat bitch off me!" She yelped, arms waving. Aaron spared me a glance, shrugged and resumed chatting with chick two. 'Bitch!" Yelled Janet. "This bitch will crack yo damn spine!" 'Oh my God Pepper! You need to fire her ass. The help is supposed to help, not attack customers." she barked all while trying to pry Janet's fingers out her hair to no avail. 'Pepper this how you doing it nigga, really?" 'Bae listen, she came on to me, I was just chillin'. You know I love you girl." Pepper hurriedly explained. Janet snorted in disbelief. 'Pepper what the hell is going on? Get her off me! Why are you just standing there instead of helping me?! You know what nigga, I'll never suck yo dick again!" The chick cried out. Man, why dat broad say that hot shit! 'Again! Again! When'd that happen? I heard yo hoe ass offer to suck his dick and now you're sayin' again! Bitch, that's my husband and this is your ass whoopin'!" Bellowed Janet, her words followed by a hard right cross. The chick would've went down if Janet wasn't still holding her hair. "Kristen, help me!" Chick two cursed and came running to help her friend, only to go sliding across the floor when I tripped her ass. Her head collided with the fridge with a resounding thud, a knot immediately formed on her big ass forehead. Shit so big its brighter than my future; shit so big she got unlimited memory. I'm just sayin' big forehead bitch. Chick one was wind milling and finally caught Janet with a punch/scratch to the cheek, digging up skin and leavin' a long bloody trail from under her right eye and stoppin' at her lip. I know that shit had to sting like hell. Janet grunted, raised her knee and slammed chick one's face against it twice. Blood gushed from her nose as Janet snatched a patch of hair out her scalp; chick one tumbled to the floor, hands cuppin' her nose. "Get off my sister!" Yelled chick two who'd finally awoke from her nap and leaped on Janet's back. Aaron and Pepper yelled in patois I don't know what, then watched in surprise when Janet flipped her ass right over her shoulder. Ole gurl landed on top of her sister in a tangle of arms and legs. "Oh shit!" Pepper shouted. "Nigga fuck you." Janet swore. "I'm sick and tired of you and yo fuckin' jump offs disrespecting me." she removed her apron and tossed it at Pepper who stood with stupid look on his face. "You can take me working here and shove it, you can take yo trash." she waved at the two girls slowly sitting up. "And do whateva tha fuck you feel, cause I'm done." Janet announced, then added a knee to Pepper's nuts before stomping away.

CHAPTER 9

I pulled up on Sigorney Street, eyes peeled for my connect and smiled when I spotted his leery, lanky ass come from behind Jerry Mack's bar which had been closed for years. Everything went on behind that mafucka. Whoever owned it would make a killin' if they charged on foot traffic. Last summer they found some dude with his head bashed in, it took the residents near Jerry's to call about the rancid smell. Three weeks later some trickin' hoe was found, leg danglin' from an over flowin' dumpster and just last month, some dude was found shot to the forehead; pockets out like bunny ears and yet dis fool was strollin' like shits cool. I flashed the lights and watched as he jogged across the street, opened the back door and slid in. 'Sup Tay?" "Shit. Why yo ass behind Jerry's fool?" Smokie chuckled, soundin' like a back firing dump truck from all the smokin' he does. "Man dat spots da happs. There's a dice game goin' right now, plus its three snow bunnies back there willin' to jump off da whole crew for that boy." Head shakin', I glared at Smokie through the rearview. "Y'all crazy, that's a jail term waitin' to happen." I tossed a rubberband stack of twenties over the seat. Smokie popped the band and started counting. "It's all dere nigga." I snapped. Smokie coughed, opened the door and spat a wad of phlegm, it landed on the back leg of some teenaged girl walkin' past. "Ole disgusting ass" I uttered. Smokie slammed the door, reached down his pants and pulled out a baggie full of different colored pills. "Really fool, you got my shit restin' by yo hot ass balls?" Smokie laughed and coughed again. "Shit, I'm trying to get yo ass near 'em but you playin' games n shit." He griped, whites of his eyes a spider web of red, starin' back at me through the mirror. "You're serious?" Smokie nodded. "Fuck yeah, yo sexy chocolate ass gets my shit hard on sight. Yo voice be raising goosebumps on a nigga." I thought about what Smokie was sayin' and inwardly smiled. "Well if and that's a big ass if, I were to take you serious, what's in it for moi?" "Dis dick up in yo guts, a nut, hell what else you need?" I smirked. "Boy please, I can get dick served up on the daily, you've gotta come better than that. Dis pussy's fat, juicy and tight; you wanna sample, pass me my money and pills. Otherwise I'll see you in two weeks." Smokie rubbed chin hairs then nodded. "Bet, drive over to Sigorney Park right quick." Turning on the car, I did as told driving up the street until the park appeared dark and gloomy on our right. Sigorney wasn't very big; it had a slide and swing set combined, about half a dozen benches and a dozen trees. Parking, I killed the lights and held my hand out palm up. Money and pills in hand, I locked 'em in the glovie, opened my door, stepped out, stretched and opened the back door. The light kicked on revealin' Smokie's naked ass dick in hand. Eight pencil thin inches. My lips curled at the thought of dat meatless dick jabbin' my uterus. Climbing in I pulled off my clothes, shimmied out panties which is hard as fuck to do inside an Altima. Smokie yanked my bra up releasing a condom I always kept for just such an occasion. "God damn," he hissed "you got some pretty tits girl." "Yeah yeah, tell me some shit I don't already know." His lips latched on while pre-cum soaked my thigh. Snatchin' up the condom I tore it open, slid it on, then gasped cause da shit fit his joint like a xxl shirt on a size extra smedium frame. "Uh..I ripped the rubber." I quickly lied, "You got one on you?" Smokie handed over a Bravo condom. "Da fuck? I'd never heard of Bravo, maybe they were for pencil dick mafuckas." Ready to end this as quickly as possible, I ripped it open, removed the 'ripped one', slid it on, climbed aboard and easily slid down it. Damn shame, shit felt like I had a Summer's Eve up my snatch. Smokie's eyes rolled as I sat still massagin' dat Vienna Sausage with pussy muscles. I threw in a few hip rolls and dis nigga yelped, tensed and skeeted all up in the condom. I started to blast his jack rabbitin' ass. Hell, my pussy ain't even get the chance to lube up good. Smokie's ass needed to go take some 'how to fuck pussy' classes for really real. "Whew! Damn gurl, dat shit was fire. Did you get yours?" He panted. Grateful for the darkness, I twisted my face, gave an eye roll and shot up the middle finger. "Hmm." I answered while thinkin', 'I sure did nigga, it's in the glove compartment." Smokie pulled his boxers and jeans up from the floor. I grabbed my panties while my kitty angrily pulsed and cursed me out for allowin' dat minute brother anywhere near her. "A'ight ma, see you in two weeks." Smokie jumped out and disappeared in the shadows. Reachin' for my dress, my fingers hit somethin' plastic. Wonderin' how the rental company could half ass clean, I pulled it from under the back of the front seat. Squinting, I couldn't make it out so I hit the light, felt my eyes widen, clicked it off and smiled. A sandwich bag filled with green stuff and I don't mean weed. It must've fallen out of Smokie's boxers. Oh well, his loss is definitely my gain. Back home I tallied up $2500 and thanked Smokie again for his generosity, even my pussy was happy. Bored, I separated my pills and put 'em into separate blank labeled pill bottles. I'd copped 30mg Morphine, 60mg Oxycodone, 15mg Hydromorphone and a couple zanies. Done, I stepped outside to flashing police lights and two officers walkin' faggy Donell to one cruiser and

Jermaine to another. Donell was yellin' and tryina break free whereas Jermaine lowered his head, not wantin' to be recognized. "Bitch ass downlow ass bastard!" Donell shouted. "This shit ain't ova! Yo ass owes me money, ain't nobody bite cho shit. I'm a dick suckin' pro-fess-ional nigga!" He continued amid the officer's rants of, 'shut up so I can read you your rights.' "You just thought cause I like dick, I'm gay and you're semi cute dat you'd get a freebie. Uh hell to the n-o fool!" The officer shoved Donell into the cruisers backseat. "Now da hood knows who and what you really are!" He got out right before the door slammed closed. Jermaine gave a fearful look around, takin' in all the faces of people he knew, some he didn't and others that loved to carry gossip; of which I'm not, I'm just sayin'. I did give a finger wave though. I knew his ass was gay, see what tryina be sneaky gets you. I wonder how his twins baby momma Sanchelle gonna react when she hears she's been ridin' and suckin' doo doo dick. Yuck! Glenda walked up Corona in hand. "Did you get that?" She whispered, like the two cruisers already at the light could hear her paro ass. "Yep, what and how many?" Glenda nervously looked around. "Let's go inside." We both headed for her door and were almost knocked over by Omar who was wavin' a gun. "Where dat drugged out bitch at!?" He barked, eyes stretched so wide it's a miracle dem shits ain't pop free and roll tha fuck away. "She who Omar?" I questioned. "Shelly's dead ass." he angrily said, spit flyin' every whicha way and shit. "Eww nigga, chill wit dat hot shit. Fuckin' wit Shel', who knows what yo spits carryin'." I snapped then wiped my cheek. Scary ass Glenda froze lookin' like a goat on crack. "Fuck you say.?" "Nigga you heard me. Why yo stupid ass keep fuckin' wit Shelly's ass when you know da outcome?" "Fuck outta here, I wasn't wit' Shelly. I was with Frankie on da benches, I had Frankie holdin' my shit in her purse. Shelly's ass must've saw it, 'cause she came outta nowhere, snatched Frankie's bag and took off." I burst out laughing 'cause I could picture Shelly's crazy ass doin' that shit. Omar probably wouldn't find her ass until every drop was gone. "Check the pink bandi on Elmer, she's probably there." ratted Glenda. "Good lookin' G." Omar smiled, tucked his gun on his waist and took off. "Why the hell you tell Omar dat shit?" "Cause her ass stole my check two months ago, so fuck Shelly. I hope Omar pistol whips her ole thieving ass." huffed Glenda before goin' inside. Chuckling, I followed her inside. "Girl, how'd Shelly steal your disability check?" I took a seat on the couch ready to munch on popcorn while listenin'. "We were outside waitin' fo' tha mailman's ass along with everyone else, just shootin' da shit. Anyway, tha mailman comes and sticks my shit in Josephine's box by accident. Since Shelly stays with her she had the keys, so she gives me my check, then asks if I want to ride to the bank with her and Josephine; I say yeah why not it beats walkin' in da heat. So after piling Josephine's wheelchair in tha backseat we're off to da bank in West Hartford 'cause Josephine had some bankin' business, I'm like wateva. So after I cashed my check I had to wait like thirty minutes for Josephine's handicapped ass, then it's back to tha car where I helped Shelly get her in the car and her chair put away. Josephine decides she wants Popeye's which is out by Walmart, so again I'm like wateva. I order and put my money back in my bra. Once we get back, I help with Josephine again, by the way, her ass might be wastin' away from congestive heart failure and Lou Gehrigs, but her ass is heavy as fuck and that wheelchair too. So I get home, reach in my bra and da shit empty." I snicker, cause her ass right about that, I'm just sayin'. "I'm searchin' like crazy but no money. It's not in front of my door, so I stomp back to Josephine's. I'm lookin' all around her car, nothing, So I snatch open the back door and there's my bank envelope, I scoop it up and the mothafuckas empty! It's empty!" I'm laughing so hard a stream of urine shot out dampenin' my panties. "Ooo girl stop. Yo stupid ass got me 'bout to pee myself!" Now Glenda's laughing too; Dove walks in eying the both of us. "Hell's so fuckin' funny? I can hear you cacklin' hoes outside." She growled, hands on hips. "Girl what bug crawled up yo rectum and is bitin' yo anus?" Glenda burst out with a laugh snorting sound. "That shit wasn't even funny. Y'all bitches high or some shit? If so, share the pot, I wanna laugh too, damn." "That reminds me." I eyed Glenda. 'What and how many? Hold yo answer til I come back, I gotta pee fuckin' wit' yo silly ass." 'Since when you all tight with Taylor's ass? Thought you didn't like or trust her?" Dove quickly questioned. 'Why you bein' such a downer? Taylor's pretty cool now that I've gotten to know her. What's your beef? Ya'll been friends a long time." Glenda was right, why was she being so uptight? She and Taylor had been cool for years, she knew how Taylor was and had accepted it, somewhat. Truthfully she was jealous, jealous of any female other than her that Taylor hung around. She waited for the day that Taylor felt for her the way she felt. 'Sorry girl I'm just tired." Dove flopped on the couch, her ass cheeks nestling right where Taylor previously sat. 'Oh yeah, Rich lookin' for you and he didn't sound too happy." Lied Dove, as Rich was lookin' for her but he just didn't know it. Taylor reappeared phone in hand. 'Y'all wanna hit up a house party with me?" 'Hell yeah." both quickly agreed. Glenda more so to draw Dove's convo away from Rich. 'Cool, make sure you bitches wear sexy shit. Make sure yo drawers and bra match and is clean, 'cause ya'll embarrass me that's yo ass." I spat grillin' both of 'em. Glenda raised her hand like a first grader. 'Let me get six, three morphine and three zanies."

CHAPTER 10

The street was packed with vehicles, some even parked up on the grass, while others were forced to walk from two streets over. The bold parked in people's driveways risking having there shit towed upon leaving the party. Dove rolled up on the curb with her old non driving ass, scraping the tire and popping off the last rim on the tire. That shit rolled down the street like a slave makin' a break for the freedom train. Glenda burst out laughin'. 'Gurl where yo ass learn to drive, Baby's R Us?" Dove sucked her teeth. 'Fuck you hoe. Tell us why Rich lookin' fo' yo ass and not in a good way. Whatchu do, take money and not deliver? Did you bite da dick? Scratch him up so that ugly wife of his knows whats up?" Dove quickly shot out. Glenda glanced at me. 'Uh, no boo. I think your confusin' me with you. I heard 'bout dem crabs you servin' up without butter and seasonin'. Want me to go with you to get it taken care of?" I almost choked on my spit, eyes waterin' from laughter. I heard Dove mutter, 'Fuck yo slow, disability havin' ass." before she rolled up on someone's yard three houses from the party; crushin' what looked like petunia's and begonia's before putting the gear in park. Gasping from Dove's words, Glenda silently got out and started walking towards a two story green and white house. Loud rap music played, people stood around smoking, drinking and talking shit to and about others as they walked up. 'Hey! You in dem green shorts!" Yelled some dude. 'Let me holler atchu!" Glenda kept walking until Dove caught a glimpse of who'd spoken and nudged Glenda so hard she stumbled and came out her shoe. The heel broke sending her straight to her knees. 'Yo Sammie, you see dat shit!" Yelled another who laughed and slapped five with his boy. Embarrassed, Glenda slowly stood, knees burning, one trickling blood, bits of grass and sod clung to her blouse. Dove screamed in pain, Glenda had punched her in the right tit. Shocked, Dove stared for a moment, titty aching, stinging and shit. 'Chill ya'll, we came to party. Hold that shit til' we leave." I turned to Glenda, happy to see her ass standin' up for herself, just not right now. 'Glenda run back to the car and put on those red heels inside my bag." Grateful, Glenda smiled, dusted her clothes and limped back to the car. 'Whatever your issue is leave dat shit right here, right now. Act up once we get inside and it's yo ass Dove, now try me." 'Jeez, okay, okay. Why yo ass buggin'? You must have a prospect waitin' inside." 'Don't worry 'bout tha fuck I got waitin' Dove. Just remember what I said." Glenda walked up and we headed inside. People milled to and fro, drinks, cigs, Black & Milds and weed in hand. Dej Loaf's 'Back Up' blared loudly, rattling windows and a few pictures on the wall as we walked through. In the kitchen I was surprised to see Roxie bartending along with some pockmark faced dude. 'Let me get a rum punch, Corona and a Bacardi and Coke." Dude nodded, quickly made my drinks and handed them over. Everyone grabbed a cup, then wandered off, so I made my way to go find Robin who was throwin' the party. Spotting trademark gear of beef and broccoli Timbs, dark blue Dickies with matching top, I walked over and smiled. 'Sup Robin?" Robin Heather cheesed as beautiful almond shaped green eyes drank me in. Her naturally curly jet black hair was worn low to the scalp, tattoos covered sixty percent of her slim frame, but the tear drops always amazed me. Some said Robin was a head honcho in the Crips gang, while others claimed it was Twenty Love. Robin never said anything and wore all colors so no one knew for sure Robin stood five feet even, but was a certified beast in the streets, her ass could give me a run. Stabbings, shootings, robbery, drugs, guns.... you name it, Robin had a hand in it. Robin gave me a hug and squeezed my ass. Oh yeah, I forgot to mention Robin liked pussy, all day, everyday. 'Hey, sexy ass Taylor in tha house." teased Robin.

"How many girls you bring?" "Two. You know I don't kick it with a bunch of bitches." "Right, right, it's cool. I got two other bitches here so these niggas should be straight. Let me show you where to change." I followed Robin upstairs, taking in an expensive living room set, tables and more put in one room. The room I stepped in had a huge bed on a raised dais surrounded by sheer white curtains. "There's a bathroom through there." Robin pointed at a partially opened door. Glancing at a woman's Rolex Robin said, "Mingle, drink, eat, whatever; the show starts at one. Oh yeah," she reached in her front pocket, pulled out a knot of cash, peeled off eight crisp hundreds. "This is for you." With a wink, she left. Pulling out my cell I texted Glenda and Dove lettin' them know everything was free and not to start any shit, then headed back downstairs where it seemed like even more people had arrived. "Taylor!" I knew that helium voice anywhere, and there she was. Sable and some white girl both dressed similar in red and white with white Nikes on. Pasting on a smile even though I now knew who the other girls were, I gave her ass a hug and air kiss. "Hey girl what you doin' here?" I asked Sable. Smiling wide, she gave a look around, no doubt countin' up the cash she'd be makin' later. "Robin invited me and a friend to dance for her birthday." She grabbed white girls hand. "This my girl Sandy aka Mink. She dances at the club too." I remembered seeing her name on the card Sable had given me.

Old girl blew a big ass bubble, then sucked it back in before saying, 'Hi, are you dancing too?" I nodded takin' the competition in. Sandy stood around five seven and was as white as newly falling snow, crystal clear blue eyes, pert nose and black girl lips I knew her ass had enhanced. 40DD's that looked like you'd crack yo jaw layin' on dem hard shits and an ass I was savin' up for. 'I know that's right!" Squealed Sable, voice high enough to break glass and makin' my ears itch. 'Get that money. Niggas wanna pass out the green, I'm damn sure gonna help myself." I hi fived Sable. 'We're gonna go look around Taylor, see you in a lil bit." With a nod, I watched 'em disappear in the mass of bodies. "There you are." said Dove walkin' up with a plate of bbq chicken, potato salad and baked beans; sauce decorating her lips. 'Girl you've gotta try this bird, the shit is delicious!" Dove yelled over the sounds of Drake's 'Hotline Bling'. I eyed her plate, it did look good, but I ain't eat shit unless I knew who'd cooked it, or sat and watched 'em make it. 'Where's Glenda?" I questioned. Dove shrugged, 'Fuck I look like, Glenda's babysitter or sum shit. I don't know, last time I saw her ass she was all hugged up with Monkey's ass." Quantavious, aka Monkey, was this midget who got big money sellin' to those eager to experience new shit, rich college kids. Monkey controlled the drugs at all the upscale colleges like Yale, Harvard and Columbia to name a few. Glancing at my watch, I peeped we had forty five minutes before shit jumped off. "We need to get ready?" A confused look on her face, Dove replied, "Ready? Get ready for what?" She polished off the last of the chicken, swiped her finger through the remaining bean sauce and sucked it off her finger so nastily some dude who'd been watchin' walked over, squeezed her ass, then stuffed a fifty in her bra before walkin' off. "For that. The chance to make some money. Robin's havin' a dance off, so I entered you, me and Glenda." "Glenda?" She snorted. "You must want to lose. Who else is dancin'?" "Sable and her girl." An ugly look slid across her face. I barely contained a smirk 'cause I knew once Dove heard Sable was not only here, but dancin' she'd give a hundred and ten percent. Sable and Dove were always in competition with each other, ever since junior high when Dove caught Sable sexin' that love of her life in the boy's locker room. They'd fight, sleep with each other's man, whatever to one up the other. Just messy. "Word, Sable hunh? Her trickin' ass don't got shit on me." she boasted. "I know girl." yeah I boosted her ego cause the team that won walked off with $2500 plus tips. I wanted that shit. The Ying Yang Twins 'Whistle While You Twerk' came through big club sized speakers, niggas started yelling and whistling. Sable and Mink walked out, Sable in a pink panty and bra set with glitter covering her body, while Mink wore a sheer white tear away leotard and pasties on her privates. Ass shakin', knee crawlin' between each other's legs; Mink even did a reverse cowgirl lap dance. I snorted 'cause if this how they give it up at the strip club, they had to be freakin' tha owner to be headliners. Big Sean's 'Ass' came on. I bounced to make sure we were lookin' right and ready to perform, cause niggas ain't wanna smell fish and musk. They were tossin' that dough, seeing that had my pussy wetter den a mafucka. Upstairs, Glenda was applying lip gloss, Dove.... Antiperspirant. 'Lord, I hope this broad don't fuck shit up cause her twat rank." 'Y'all ready?" 'Hell yeah! I need that dough now that I put Bernard's punk ass out." spat Dove. 'Ditto. Rich ass actin' shiesty so I can definitely use it." Pulling off my clothes, their eyes widened lettin' me know a bitch looked damn good, always. Haters remember that shit. Just as we hit the bottom of the stairs, Freak Nasty's 'Da Dip' came on hypin' the crowd. Dove crawled through the crowd archin' her back, wigglin' her ass and even sniffin' a few crotches. Glenda started twerkin' then slow motioned it. Money rained down and as I strutted in wearin' a tiny ass private school skirt and two pasties, whistles rang out. Glenda and Dove started rubbin' and kissin' each other while I bent over, flipped up my skirt, did a back flip, then a scissor and came back up my feet surrounded by nothin' less than fifties.

CHAPTER 11

I made out like a bandit at Robin's party, two racks; Glenda and Dove made $1100. Needless to say when it came down to it, my team did the damn thang. Anyhoo, the Courts decided to throw a cookout, citing everyone who wanted to eat had to bring somethin'. So I grabbed some no name liter sodas and made my way to the back where tables and grills were set up. Immediately my stomach growled from the smell of ribs, hamburgers and chicken grilling. Jacko worked the grills, his beer belly hanging out the bottom of his shirt, stretch marks and nappy belly hair on display. Now normally I ain't eating shit Jacko prepared, seein' as how he always had a finger up his nose that found its way in his mouth; but the booger eatin' bastard had on gloves, so I decided to chance it, I'm just sayin'. Jacko was the hood repairman, be it a washing machine or a starter for your car, Jacko was your man. It was crazy though, cause his ass didn't even live in the Courts. He lived in East Hartford, but made his way there faithfully, every morning. Looking around, I spotted Shelly eying possible vics, guess Omar hadn't caught up with her ass yet. Okra and Marcus were sharin' a forty ounce, Rosalie and her dick sharin' daughters, along with a host of other residents; there were even a few people from the apartment buildings across the street. Walkin' up to the table I set the sodas down, felt someone starin' and slowly looked around, tryina spot who was getting' there stare on; when my eyes collided with this dude whom I've never seen before. My eyes drank in a six three caramel toned, flawless complexion, low haircut with deep waves, thick shapely brows with light brown eyes. An aquiline nose, a thin mustache, firm suckable lips, a nice frame encased in Levi's and a white tee with the Levi logo across the chest. My eyes lowered to see the new black and grey Jordan's on size twelve feet. He stood next to annoyin' ass David. You ever knew someone who as soon as they opened their mouth yo eyes got to rollin', anger bubbled and you wanted to punch 'em in the face? Well that's David's ass. Its sad 'cause David's ass is sexy, he's a young thug with a Jerimih face. Ump, I'd do his lil nineteen year-old ass right god damn it! David nudged tha cutie upon seein' me givin' him the once over. I couldn't hear what was said, as someone hooked up their house speakers and Lil Wayne's 'Lollipop' started playin'. Ahh the classics. Fuck it, I strode over to David intent on learnin' everythin' about sexy caramel. 'Hey

Taylor, sup momma? You lookin' good as always." David licked his lips. "When you gone give yo boy a taste like everybody else? I'm askin' cause you sleepin' on a nigga's skills out here. Have yo ass lookin' for me with binoculars." See what I mean. All dat shit wasn't necessary; that's exactly why his ass will never get as he put it, a taste. Ignorin' David's ass before he flipped the switch, I smiled and stuck out my hand. "Hi I'm Taylor and you are?" Them dreamy light browns smoothly took in my peach cami top and white figure hugging capris and the bunion, corn free pedicured toes on display. He smiled, a dimple winked in his cheek while straight pearly whites shone in the noonday sun. "Kione, Kione Fyne." my smile widened. "You damn sure are." "Yo son! She wantchu!" David screamed while jumpin' in place. "Yo dog, they call her an old freak 'cause she be givin' up da pussy and turnin' dudes out my nigga!" Frownin' dat switch jiggled cause he was fuckin' pushin' it. "Yo David man, chill." said Kione, his smooth, sexy deep toned voice sendin' shivers down my damn spine. Tsk, ain't no nigga ever EVER done that. I couldn't wait to slob and ride on that Mr. Goodbar. My eyes dropped, zoomin' in on da dick print slightly visible, my mouth went dry. "Sorry, sorry." David quickly said, his own beady ass eyes zoomin' in on my breasts. If his ass saw my nipple he'd probably cum in his boxers, fuckin' annoyin' ass! "Nice to meet you Taylor, and may I say you are one beautiful black woman."

Now I started to read his ass cause why can't I be a beautiful woman without the black tossed in the middle; but then I pictured myself ridin' his tongue and let the shit go. 'Aww shit! Man she lickin' dem joints, got my shit hard imagining what else she gone lick." 'Nigga shut yo virgin ass up!" I snapped, I really didn't want Kione to see me act out of character so soon, but I'd had enough of David. 'You wanna know why I ain't tryina get with yo ass? It's cause you loud, ignorant and think everything's a fuckin' joke. Nigga you'll never see, sniff or taste these goodies; unless you snatch a pair of my panties. Now get the fuck away from me for I tell da hood how you come faster than a rocket nigga." Stunned, David stared at me all hard, like he wanted to slap a bitch, please. I'd cut his ass from A to Z, and not think nothin' of it. 'Fuck outta here." David spat and gripped his Johnson. 'My shit works well, ask Roberta 'bout mines." 'Don't need to." I kindly interrupted, 'Roberta done already shared about yo curler width, cum all quick dick." David's jaw fell, noticin' a few eyes on him David muttered, 'Fuck y'all! I don't want yo old ass pussy no way" and stomped off like da bitch he is. 'Sorry 'bout dat Kione, but some mafuckas can't take rejection and need to be put in da pocket." 'No, I apologize. Sometimes Dave doesn't know when enough's enough." Smiling, I batted lashes gaving him another look over and estimated him to be around twenty-six; a year over my limit but for his sexy ass I'd make an exception. 'So Taylor where's your man?" He asked, 'Same place he's been for the last thirty some odd years, prison." Hell, wasn't no shame in my game. I mean why lie when he could ask anyone round here 'bout me and they'd tell his ass the same thang. 'Oh word, so you free and clear hunh?" I nodded, smile wide, nipples hard, pussy moist. 'And you, you here wit' yo girl, baby momma, fuck partner, wife?" I threw out, trying to cover all bases. Kione laughed, even that shit was sexy. Man I couldn't wait to snack on his sexy frame. 'Nah ma, I'm single, none of what you mentioned. No kids either." his eyes lingered between my legs. 'Although makin' 'em are half the fun." I felt my cheeks swell from another smile. My phone rang again and again. I ignored Smokie's blowin' up my cell havin' ass. I guess he finally realized he'd left his shit behind. That's what he gets for putting pussy over dough. I pushed talk. 'Sup Smokie? I'm not due to call you until Friday; unless you're callin' to tell me you get some new shit in stock." Smokie snorted. 'Hell naw! I been blowin' yo shit up for seven days yo. Bring me my shit or that's yo ass Taylor." warned Smokie. 'Smoke, what tha hell are you talkin' about? What shit boy? And don't be threatenin' me nigga. I've been busy, ain't nobody avoidin' yo seven day stalkin' ass. I figured yo ass wanted another go round and I was too tied up to deliver." 'Yo ass gone be tied up if you don't run me mines!" He blared. I chuckled.

'Smoke we both know yo ass ain't doin' shit. How many times you got ganked by dem white boys and ain't do shit, chalk it up boo." Fuck it, I was done pretendin'. Smokie wasn't gonna do shit but blow a bunch of smoke, get it. 'Word. You talkin' a lotta shit for someone with a death wish. It's all good yo, watch yo back." The line went dead. 'Fuckin' loser." I uttered. 'How you mad when you dropped yo shit? I ain't pick yo pocket, that's the game boo; mafuckas get got on the daily." Done with thinkin' 'bout Smokie and his wack ass threats, my cell rang again, Ty. 'Hey lover." I purred, feelin' my kitty moisten. 'Sup?" the mechanized voice said. 'You sexy. Is this the call I've been waitin' for?" Ty chuckled. 'Yeah baby, come see a nigga." 'Give me an hour boo." 'Fone." Call ended, I went to shower. Anger had his eyes fiery red as he sat inside his car, his possessions loaded in trunk and backseat. Hatred had his hands choking the steering wheel as he watched his loving and devoted wife Mary direct the movers on removing his huge TV, leather furniture, bar and more from his man cave. After twenty-five years of marriage it was over. Mary had even called his job of thirteen years and told anyone who'd listen that he was a liar and a cheater, who'd squandered their life savings on pussy. Somehow those words got back to his boss who'd ordered a surprise audit of his department and voila! Destruction and chaos as it came to light, he'd been filtering funds for his own pleasure and had been fired on the spot and told that the law would come calling. "All of this was those bitches fault." thought Rich as he stared into space remembering the day shit went left. Meanwhile... Legs spread interstate wide, I gripped Ty's melon as his tongue tap danced along my clit so damn good, juices poured down my ass crack. Not missin' a beat, Ty dove in and licked that up too. Images of Kione's fine ass had me wet as fuck as Ty smacked and slurped. "Gotdamn Ki..Ty, eat dat pussy. Sss." my ass lifted chasin' the orgasm I felt approachin', my eyes slammed shut. I knew my face was all discombulated, ya'll know what I mean. The 'cum face' was in full effect. "Ahh fuck!" slid out as I shook and shivered in pleasure. Ty slid up my body his dick hot, hard and oozin' pre-cum along the way. "Damn." Ty grunted, my walls squeezed and gripped while my hips undulated. "Shit girl, yo pussy the best." Ty said. Inwardly smilin' I threw it back, rolled and got on top 'cause I needed to feel every inch of the dick... Meanwhile... Rich could clearly hear Mary's yells as he drove, could feel the paper from her Gyn doctor smacking him in the face, its edge leaving a paper cut over his eyebrow that stung like hell. Anger festered churning into rage as he neared his destination. Herpes with a side dish of crabs, acrimony ate at his soul turning into a putrid abomination of loathing so deep he needed retribution in the worse way. Rich parked, barely noting the people or scent of grilling food in the air as he strode across tufts of grass and dirt, littered with empty snack bags, cigarette butts and a few liquor bottles. Tunnel vision set in as he neared her door, his dick hardening at the thought of wrapping his hands around her throat and squeezing until the whore's eyes popped out. Rich tried the door, finding it unlocked caused a drip of pre-cum to leak free. Closing the door, Rich silently crept through living room, then kitchen with no success on finding his target. His face darkened, then he heard it, the flush of a toilet. A demonic grin across snarling lips, Rich crept upstairs; his two hundred plus frame feeling lightweight. Her stairs were even on his side as they remained quiet under his girth. Glenda, nose wrinkled from the acrid smell coating the air, grabbed the half empty can of orange scented air freshner, and started spraying. "Got damn." Glenda grunted, reached back, flushed and exhaled. Eating Okra's cabbage had her asshole on fire and her stomach cramping something terrible. Taylor and Dove had snuck off to do their usual fuckery. "Bitches could've invited me." uttered Glenda followed by a scream horror flick worthy. "You fuckin' disease ridden bitch! I warned yo nasty ass...I warned you!" screamed Rich, spit flew pelting Glenda in the face. Ass cheeks slippery from not having the chance to wipe, Glenda jumped up heart damn near gallopin' from her chest cavity. "R..Rich, what, uh..what are you doin't here?" Stammered out, taking in Rich's unkempt look and wild bloodshot eyes glaring evilly at her. She swallowed a sudden knot in her throat. "You ruined my life you whorin' slut, you gave me herpes bitch and now you'll pay!" Glenda felt her heart drop between shitty asscheeks, raised the can she still held and frantically sprayed Rich in his fat ass face. Rich screamed and grabbed his face. Seeing her chance, Glenda fled from the bathroom, then choked on a scream when the stairs rushed up to greet her. Down she went, back and ankle taking the brunt of her fall. Landing with a thud, Glenda moaned as her vision faded in and out and her ears rang. Rich, panting leaned down and started punching her everywhere, followed by kicks and stomps that forced excrement from her body. Her eyes immediately swelled, a loud crunch sounded when a rib snapped, two teeth went flying before Rich panicked upon hearing voices nearby and fled out the back door. "Glenda! What's takin' you so long? I thought you were gonna walk.. aahh!" Screamed Rosalie, who'd just spotted Glenda's ass laid out bleeding and unconscious on the floor. Walking closer, something crunched under her foot. Looking down, Rosalie realized she'd stepped on two teeth. "Oh shit, are you dead girl?" Whispered Rosalie. "My bad. If yo ass dead, you sure as hell can't answer." Glenda moved and Rosalie screamed, then ran for her life.

CHAPTER 12

I couldn't believe it. Earlier when I made it back home the Court was in an uproar. At first I thought I missed a major brawl between the Holmes and Peter's families. Every summer they got shit poppin', even the youngest at seven would scrap; but then Rosalie, actin' all distraught, ran up and told me some incredible shit. Glenda was in the hospital after someone beat the pure T hell out her ass. She'd discovered Glenda and had called the law, unbeknownst at the time she'd also helped herself to some of Glenda's shit before doing so. So I called Dove, had her come scoop me and we made our way over to Hartford Hospital. And now here we stood, lookin' at Glenda who was truly fucked up. Three broke ribs, her right leg broke in two places and would require pins and shit to stabilize. A bruised spleen, two teeth knocked out, a concussion and a black eye. Damn! Someone knocked her the fuck out! Dove took in

Glenda's injuries and begin to fidget, before takin' a seat, only for her leg to start jumpin'. 'Fuck wrong with chu?" Shit, she was making me nervous. 'Uh..nothin'. Why you comin' at me like I know sumthin?" barked Glenda, soundin' guilty as fuck. My brow arched, arms akimbo, I glared at her nervous fingernail bitin' ass. 'What!" Came out kinda loud, Glenda stirred and gave a painful moan. Quickly walkin' bedside, I clasped Glenda's hand that was free of IV's and gave a soft rub. Bein' here brought back painful memories, memories I fought to keep at bay. 'Glenda, can you hear me? Squeeze my hand if you can hear me?" Dove snorted. 'Her ass unconscious, doped up on meds. Of course her ass can't hear you." I gave her ass tha middle finger and glanced back at Glenda who still appeared as if she hadn't heard, so I turned on Dove's sneaky behind. 'Spill it." Dove's triflin' ass looked at the TV, the iv pole, Glenda and everything else; til' I tightly grabbed dat hoes jaw and gave a squeeze so firm and tight I left three fingerprints behind. 'I'mma ask yo ass again before I leave yo halfwit body in that extra bed visitin' Glenda." Dove stiffened, sagged in her seat and started ballin', that bullshit ain't faze me as I waited on her to spit it out. 'Okay, okay." she sniffed wiped her nose with her sleeve, then glanced up through damp lashes. 'Bitch please, I taught yo triflin' butt dat move now spill it." The switch jiggled, I felt kind of bad cause Glenda had a learnin' disability and wouldn't be in that bed if I hadn't occasionally let her ass hang and put her up on game. Dove giggled and wiped her eyes. "Right, I forgot I was taught by the master of manipulation." "Hmm, was that sarcasm I heard?" I balled a fist, ready to knock her in the face to show her I wasn't fuckin' around and wanted answers right damn now. I guess Dove realized what it is, 'cause she quickly started talkin'. "Rich mad. He blames Glenda, he did this crazy shit." "And how you know this?" "You know Rich be trickin'. Shit I took you when Glenda stood him up. Anyway Rich got burnt, his wife on a yearly check-up got the bad news and as she's a faithful woman," Dove threw up quotation marks. "she knew off rip who infected her. She confronted Rich, put him out and even called his job. Once they found out, they did a department audit, saw what Rich had been up to and fired his fat ass with the promise of impending jail time to come." Deriding look in place I ice grilled Dove. "And how'd you hear all this?" Momentarily stuck, I could see Dove's wheels churning as she thought of how and what to say in answer. "I heard. You know the streets love to talk, a mafucka can't shut da hell up." I knew her ass like the back of my neck, she was lyin' most likely she'd talked to Rich and told him some bullshit. I suddenly remembered Dove mentioning Rich was lookin' for Glenda. "Hmm, where's Rich now? Hidin' at yo place?" "Hell naw! I don't wanna be anywhere near Rich now, or ever. I hope they catch and lock his crazy ass up." She stated. "If I find out you had anythin' to do with.." Dove jumped up all swole and junk like I'm gonna cower from dis hoe and laughed dead in my face. "I wish yo ass would hoe. I ain't tagged you in a while, but there's always plenty of space and opportunity anytime you ready." I calmly told her ass, switch jiggling. I watched as that bitch calculated, weighin' tha pros and cons of riskin' tryin' my ass; defeat slid in her eyes. I knew Dove ain't have it in her. She might be sneaky, convivin' and full of shit, but her ass knew how far to take things when it came to moi. Arrivin' home, I was shocked to see Omaire waitin' on me. We hadn't talked and set up a date, so seeing him instead of his driver Jarvis had me stuck for a quick sec. Dove took one look at Omaire's money green Porsche and creamed her panties. "Omg! Gurl do you see that sexy ass car?" she gushed. "The owner of that pretty bitch could fuck me any way he wants." "Girl please." I retorted. "Who hasn't already done that." Dove rolled her eyes, gave herself the once over, patted her hair, fixed her pink jean mini and said, "How I look? Never mind Tay', let me go introduce myself to my new man." and strutted towards the Porsche. "Gone girl, do you!" I called, givin' Dove enough space to play her cards while slowly followin'. I watched as the driver's door swung open and out stepped Omaire's stutterin' self. "Hey handsome, can I help you with anything? I mean anything at all." she stressed. Omaire's eyes swung in my direction and a smile formed. "M..m...maybe." Dove reared back like he'd slapped the spit out her mouth. Her smile grew. "Well say no more handsome." 'Please don't.' Dove silently ruminated, 'Cause I'm liable to laugh in yo face.' Omaire smiled showin' off the gold and platinum mouthpiece with fangs he'd copped earlier on display. Dove felt pussy juices drip at the sight. "Wh.. wha..what's your n..name be..beautiful?" Smile so wide all thirty-two were showin', dollar signs in her eyes. Dove swiftly took in cream colored Alfred Fiandace slacks and baby blue short sleeved button up. Stuart Weitzman loafers on size twelve feet, but his jewelry, an Audemars Piquet watch and six carat diamond pinky ring had her ready to propose marriage. "I'm Dove handsome; and like my name I'm strong, sexy, beautiful and would make a lucky man the perfect mate. Can I have my future mates name?" I edged closer. "Omaire." Dove licked plump lips. "My number is 993-5745, call me handsome. Trust, once you do you'll never need another." "Y..you w..wild ma." Dove winked. "You have no idea." she flirted. I walked up, side stepped Dove and right into Omaire's arms; greetin' him with a kiss and a whole lotta tongue action. Omaire eagerly returned the kiss, his hands roamed down to my ass where he cupped and squeezed before coming up for air; eyes alit with hunger. "Hey boo." I purred. "To what do I owe the pleasure of your visit?" I could hear Dove stomp her feet and curse under her breath

"Hmm, don't hate boo. Watch and learn when in the presence of a master, I'm just sayin." Before Omaire could answer, I pulled slightly away, turned and with wide smile made the intro. "Dove this my good friend Omaire. Omaire this my home gurl Dove." Jealousy shone like a beacon from Dove's eyes as they glared at me, then Omaire. "Yeah we've met." she said, lips on pout, "I..I want y..you t..to come for d..dinner." stammered Omaire, breakin' the tension coloring the air. "Am I welcome too?" Dove cut in. Omaire glanced at me tryin' to discern if invitin' her was okay but I kept the blank face, 'cause he wasn't shit to me but dick, dollas and gifts. "Uh, s..sure." Dove beamed. "Great!"

CHAPTER 13

Fuck dat, I'm ready to show Taylor's ass that she ain't the only one who can pull a nigga with money. After tonight she might as well lose Omaire's fuckin' digits, 'cause he'll belong to me and I for damn sure ain't sharin'. After catchin' Bernard and Aisha's ass fuckin' in Glenda's bathroom, I cursed Glenda's ass out for not givin' a heads up. Made her make it up to me by eatin' my pus' and hookin' me and Rich up. Then I kicked Bernard's ass out, called his raggedy ass mom dukes, told her the scoop on her dirty dick son while playin' tha distraught girlfriend and asked if she'd keep Jeff for a few weeks while I got my thoughts together. She said yes and trust, I dropped Jeff off so damn fast I had to go back five days later with clothes for him. Hell, I was on a mission. If I could forget about flesh and blood and get Glenda beat down, Taylor's ass didn't stand a chance if it were somethin' I really wanted; and I wanted s..s..stuttering a..a..ass Omaire. Pussy creamin' at the sight of Omaire's huge fuckin' crib, I drove through the open gate, smirk on my face 'cause I'd intentionally left Taylor's ass back in Hartford; which would give me all night to get what I want, Omaire. Marvelin' at miles of green grass, statues, some with water drippin' and all kinds of flowers, I pulled into the circular driveway; eyes wide at the sight of luxury vehicles on display. Shit, if Omaire got shit twisted, there appeared to be quite a bounty to pick and choose from. Parked, my jaw dropped when an older white dude dressed like a penguin opened my door and assisted me out. Well damn, a bitch could get use to that shit. 'Good evening madam, right this way." he politely stated his accent, English I think. It was Kinda sexy. Too bad he was ugly, 'cause I'd break him off on accent alone. Smiling bright I followed Ole E inside and gasped. Beautiful chandliers with what looked like gold trimming, shiny floors so clean I could eat off dem shits; we passed furniture so plush I know it would feel like I'd sat on pure fluffy clouds. Gorgeous artwork hung on the walls along with others were sittin' on mini stands. Dude led me into what he called the 'sitting room' where a bunch of mofos mingled, some smokin' cigars I knew weren't cheap by the smell; snifter of fine liquor in hand, while the women sipped wine and shit. 'Would madam like a drink?" 'Sure, let me get a beer." dude frowned like I insulted his ass or somethin'. 'No beer madam." 'Look stop with the madam shit, call me T..Dove," She quickly corrected.

Yeah she started to set off a whole buncha ignorant shit usin' Taylor's name. "Of course." he sniffed like he smelt a fart, "We have the finest white and red wines, Pinot Noir, Macallan Single Malt Whiskey or I can have a Mint Julep or Ono Cocktail made for you." Dove smacked her lips. "Fine, I'll take that Macaulay Culkin on ice." Dude smirked, nodded and walked over to a bar I hadn't noticed. "H..hello everyone, g..glad you could m..make it." hearin' Omaire bought a smile on and he looked damn good in a black and teal Emilio suit, yum! "Omaire, its about time you made an appearance. It always did take you hours to get dressed." teased an older woman with lightly salted hair. Jewels decorated her throat and fingers while an ocean blue fitted L'Wren Scott covered her frame. "M..mom when did y...you g..get here?" He asked, smiling bright. "About an hour ago and yes, I know your father is coming. I'll try and be on my best behavior." Omaire pulled her in for a hug. "Where's Carlton?" "Mexico, he sends his apologies for being unable to attend." Omaire nodded, noticed Dove and made his way over, palms sweating. She watched until he stood right before her smelling of Giorgio. "Y.. you m..made it." "Sure did. You have a elegant home." "Thanks," Omaire gave a quick look around, "w..where's T..Taylor?" She shrugged, 'cause Dove could give a fuck, she prayed her ass never showed. A Hispanic chick, dressed in a maid's uniform walked in, whispered somethin' to Ole E, who made his way around the room with a tray of drinks. "W..why don't y..you all introduce y..yourselves while I m..make sure d..dinner is r..ready." said Omaire, giving Dove's body, encased in tight white halter dress another glance before exiting. His mother stood, tapped the side of her glass with a big ass diamond ring and spoke. "Hello everyone, my name is Kitty Fredericks and our handsome host is my son Omaire. Please introduce yourselves." "The names Tommy Gaines, I'm a music producer." said a reed thin black man with a handlebar mustache. "I'm Nathan King. I'm executive producer at Kwane Records." said a tall, white man with blazing red hair. "I'm Natalie Ervin; I'm a voice coach," said a heavyset white woman. "My name is Dove Mitchell and I'm a friend of Omaire." Dove told the dinner guests, then felt her jaw drop and heart race when in walked none other than Kidd! Omg, the rapper Kidd was a dinner guest! She barely noticed the Oriental chick on his arm, her tactics immediately switched from Omaire to Kidd. And damn was he sexy! "Sorry I'm late." Kitty snorted, then rolled her eyes at Kidd's date who was cute by the way; just not cuter then Dove. She stood a dimutive five one and probably weighed a buck o five. With waist length jet black hair, slanted eyes, button nose and full lips. Eyes lowered, Dove took in a body she knew her ass hadn't been born with; 36 26 36. Yeah right, ole slanty eyed bitch. "I'm Omaire's father Omaire Sr. and this is my fiancée Ming Xiang."

"Hello." she greeted and Dove wanted to fuckin' gag. Omaire returned, "Okay, right t..this w..way I hope y..your hungry, m.. my chef Manuel w..whipped u..u..up some delicious items." Just as everyone was seated, Dove on Omaire Jr.'s left, who comes speed walkin' in? Taylor's skank ass. Teeth grindin', Dove grilled her ass, lips curled in distaste. Her ass was dolled the hell up too, old bitch tryina out do her. Not! Her hair was twisted up in a chignon, somethin' they teased uppity white bitches about all the time; with curly wisps danglin' around nape and ears. A form fittin' off the shoulder butter yellow Gianfranco Ferre knee length dress, shit she'd never see da hoe wear looked good. Bitch, even her feet were snazzy in Max Azria stilettos, and was that Agent Provocateur she smelled? Oh dis hoe done pulled out all da moves. Servers wheeled out four carts loaded with food that had her stomach growlin'. Medium rare filet mignon, she knew that cause dude next to her moaned and started lickin' his chops when he saw it. Some sort of antipasta with chicken, chicken scaloppini, which Kitty announced was her favorite, or again Dove would've been clueless. Szechwan crusted salmon with stir fry veggies in garlic oyster sauce. Da fuck? Where tha black food. Like fried chicken? Fried fish? She saw turkey thighs which looked promisin' until the chef poured a white wine that looked like some type of sauce, eww! Next! Pernil, which was roasted pork flavored with garlic, vinegar and oregano and last oxtails with pigeon peas and rice, now that she could eat. "M..mom, dad, I have a..a surprise for y..you." and out walked some chick, Omaire Sr. jumped out his seat, raced around the table and embraced her. "Aww hell naw!" Taylor yelled, also jumped up and swung knockin' da lady into one of tha carts sendin' food everywhere. Jaw dropped, Dove stared in astonishment. Did she miss somethin' here, cause Taylor had swung like she was tryina take ole gurls head off. Kidd grabbed her ass in a bear hug while the vocal coach screamed like her ass was bein' attacked. "Yo! I don't know, nor care who you are, but that's my mothafuckin' sista you just clocked. You would wanna chill before I handle yo ass, real talk!" Blared Kidd who'd went from talkin' all whitish to niggerish in the blink of an eye. Dove held her laughter cause she didn't wanna be kicked out and tha show was just beginnin'. She calmed down, somewhat, watchin' some dude with a crazy mustache help Doris to her feet; while an older woman who favored Omaire Jr. laughed until tears ran. "Now I'ma let you go, but chill da fuck out. I ain't got no problem chokin' tha shit out cho pretty ass." Givin' a subtle nod I choked and wheezed as air shot down my throat and back into lungs previously bereft of air. "T..Taylor, the f..f..fucks goin' on?!" Omaire loudly stuttered. "Can I talk to you in private?" I asked Omaire, 'cause I could see Dove's nosy ass out the corner of my eye soakin' in the happs. Omaire nodded, I fell in step and left the room. Ump,

Dove sipped her Macaulay Culkin so glad she'd attended Omaire's dinner, eyes swiveled to Omaire Sr. and his sister who he kneeled before, damp napkin blottin' her nose, which continued to leak blood. "You okay sis?" She nodded, sniffed and glanced at her green blouse which had turned brown in some spots from blood, "Doris, why did Omaire's date punch you?" Dove sat her glass down so fast it clattered against her fork, eyes swung in her direction, no doubt takin' in a pissed face. Since when had that hot shit been determined? "She's just a mean, hateful woman." 'Right.' thought Dove while listenin' to Doris whine like she was so hurt. She almost choked on the curse clawin' her throat. Taylor had shit with her, but she could clearly see ole Doris was on tha bull. Kitty cleared her throat. "Oh Doris, please cut it out. You're being your usual overly dramatic self. I'm positive that young lady had a very good reason for punching you in your face the way she did." said Kitty. pleased look on her face at seeing Doris attacked. "Kitty not now. Can't you see Doris is in pain. She's upset and rightly so and doesn't need to be interrogated." spat Kidd while Ming sat, calmly sipping a cocktail, her thoughts on her Hispanic lover. "Its okay Omaire." Doris patted his cheek, "Kitty has always been selfish and more concerned with herself, that's the reason your marriage didn't last." "What!" Yelped Kitty. "My marriage didn't last because you ran and told Omaire a bunch of untruths. Personally I think you wanted him for yourself and still do." Doris jumped up. 'How dare you insinuate such a disgusting thing! That's my brother, who I love very much and you're right, I did run and tell; that his wife was sleeping with the groundskeeper!" The guests gasped and nervously looked among themselves. Taylor and Omaire walked in hand in hand, Omaire with a sated look upon his face. "What's goin' o..on?" Kitty angrily paced while hatefully staring at Doris. "Nothing dear. Are you and your young lady alright?" Goofy grin in place, Omaire pulled Taylor close and chuckled. "Yeah, w..we're good ma." Kitty gave a pleased smile, while Dove stewed in her seat. "Great, now can we continue with dinner, I for one am starving after that long flight."

CHAPTER 14

"Girl don't yo ass ever stay home and sleep in," I complained as Dove came through the door. It had been two weeks since Omaire's dinner with Dove's ass actin' shiesty as fuck during the interim. "Whateva. It's eleven, yo ass should be up. Anyway, Glenda's bein' discharged, she wants me to pick her up; figured you'd wanna ride." "A'ight, let me get dressed." An hour later, 'cause beauty can't be rushed, we walked into Glenda's room where she sat on the bed, dressed and ready to go. "Hey y'all. Thanks for comin' to get me." Ten minutes later, Glenda was discharged and we're cruisin' down the Avenue, when I spot Doris' ass goin' into Peppers. "Pull ova Dove, I want a beef patty." With a mumble, Dove jumped into the other lane, amid blaring horns and double parked. "Hurry up and grab me one too, with a coco bread and a Sprite!" She yelled as I slammed the door, jogged across the street and inside Peppers. I didn't see Aaron or Janet, but some young boy worked the register, so I assumed Pepper was in the back. Doris stood at the counter, her back facing me, while two other custies eyed the board listed with the daily specials and more. Wicked grin and sparklin' eyes, I walked up and punched that bitch dead in the back of her head so hard I heard her neck crack like I was a chiropractor. Her forehead smacked the counter. 'Oh shit!" Yelled a female customer. She whipped out her cell and started recording the beatdown on Doris. Her ass tried to fight me back, but that shit wasn't gonna fly. I beat that ass til' counter boy snapped awake, hopped over the counter and yanked me off her ass. 'Told you I'd beat cho ass everytime I see yo ass bitch!" I yelled switch on high. 'How you like me now hoe?!" I spat, ready to stomp her ass if she even remotely looked like she was tunin' her lips to say some shiesty shit. Pepper came flyin' out the back, hands coated in flour. 'Wha da raas gwan!" He bellowed, then eyed me and cursed. 'Me should'a known." Laughing, I gave Pepper a hug. 'Sorry Pep', but when an ass whooping calls, I must answer." Doris finally gathered her bearings, stood and dazedly looked around as blood dripped from her nose. She grimaced, showing blood stained teeth while her eye was swiftly closing. With a last look around, Doris stumbled from Peppers. Of course I forgot Dove's food and had to hear her damn mouth the whole ride home, until I told her ass why I'd really gone into Pepper's. That garnered a whole new rack of questions; like, Why did I fight her at Omaire's? How did I know Doris and what was my beef with her? Blah, blah, blah. How 'bout bitch 'cause I wanted to? How 'bout cause lookin' at her mugly ass made me want to clock her one good time? How 'bout if Dove didn't shut tha hell up, I'd be clockin' her ass too? My cell rang. Seein' a number I didn't recogonize I started to send it to voicemail, then pressed talk. "Sup." "Hello, may I speak to Taylor?" I didn't know the voice and a bill collector definitely wouldn't be callin' me Taylor, although if it were, dude sounded good. "This is she." "It's Kione, how you doin' ma?" Smilin', I shot Dove a look cause her nosy ass was all up in my fridge. Her ass knew I ain't play that shit. If her pussy smelled like a lion's ass who knew what was on dem mitts, I'm just sayin'. "I'm fine and yourself?" I asked. Dove pulled out a quart of orange juice flipped the top and chugged from the spout, my back teeth ground together at the sight. Oohh I wanted to pluck her in the forehead with a spatula. "What do you think?" Damnit, I missed what Kione had asked. "Sorry, can you repeat that? My cell's reception had faded out." Chucklin', Kione repeated the words. "I'm in the Courts, I wanna see you. What you think?" My twat meowed, hot damn. Hell to tha yess come thru boo and hit me off with the deathstroke, I'm just sayin. "Sure, I'm in building nine; apartment 2916." "See you in ten." Cheesing, I hung up, bounced up and strode into the kitchen where dis trick stood munchin' on my leftover cat and rice; I mean sweet n sour chicken from Red Star. "Hoe, I hope yo hands ain't leavin' traces of dick juice all over my fuckin' fridge. And did you ask me if you could eat my damn Chinese food? If I see one shit kernel I'm takin' it to yo fuckin' face." I quickly promised. Dove rolled her eyes, and the switch jiggled. "Whateva Tay', my hands as clean as yo snatch hoe." my brow arched. "Aha ha, you got jokes. You wish yo shits were half as clean as dis good ole snatch." I patted my pride and joy. "Cause we both know you're the queen of infectious diseases. Matter of fact, did yo ass ever make it to the free clinic to cure those crabs? Oops, nope cause I see dem shit crawlin' from here." Bam! Dove blanched, twisted her lips and stuck up her middle finger like that shit fazed me. "Why you always comin' at me all types of crazy? We supposed to be girls, besties." "Bitch please." I smacked my lips. "Yo ass always tryina do me, then when I come fo' yo ass you wanna whine, cry and moan dat always me crap." I spat, eyin' her bi polar ass. A knock sounded and that quick the switch was off and my mood was back where it should be, on tha dick at the door. "Who's got yo ass cheesin'?" "Nonya." I replied and swung the door open, my tongue damn near got stuck to the roof of my mouth at the sight of all that luscious man meat standin' before me. Ump, ump, ump! Kione had my mouth dry and salivatin' at the same damn time okay. Nipples so hard as they pressed against my top. Da shits ached, while my kitty soaked my boy shorts I'd slid on minus any panties. Jeezus let me find eleven fat inches I can barely get my mouth around and I'll be foreva grateful. Oh and Lord, let him know how to work me so I can cum a rack of times! Amen. Kione wore blue jean shorts, showin' off slightly bowed legs, his ankle socked feet were shoved into Nike slippers, his upper frame covered by a wifebeater that had my heart skippin'. Something about his ass had me fienin' like never before. "Well hello there." purred Dove, eying Kione with hunger in her gaze. Please, tha nigga wanted a meal not a damn can of salmon and crackers. Dis bitch right here! Ignorin' Dove's ole cum thirsty ass, I pulled Kione inside, shoved Dove out and slammed the door amid her comments of 'I'm scared she's a triple threat.' Bullshit. With a grunt, I yanked the door open so fast I almost tore my arm out the socket. "Bitch I ain't neva scurred. You think you can pull him?" I waved an arm. "Come on in." Kione, with a confused look in place watched our interaction before smiling. "Not at all." said Dove. "Jus' a lil girl talk is all. I'm Dove, Tay's bestie and you are?" Kione shook her hand. "Kione, nice to meet you Dove. I like yo name, it's different." Dove damn near melted. Ugh could her ass be anymore fake. "Thank you. So are you Tay's new man?" Kione rubbed his jaw and smirked. "Nah, we're just gettin' to know each other." Dove nodded.

"Okay and how yo girl feel 'bout that?" Again I remained quiet. "I don't have one. If I did I wouldn't be here. You got a man shorty?" Dove giggled. "Nah, none of those. Once you make a nigga yo man they end up changin' on a bitch. The shit ain't worth tha aggravation." "Right, right. Maybe you haven't met the right dude." Said Kione. "That's all well and good, but for now I just wanna have fun. Think you can help a girl out with that?" Again Kione looked my way, as if tryina figure out was this some sort of trick. "Uh nah, sorry. I'm interested in yo girl Taylor." Dove's face fell revealin' a momentary mask of hate and jealousy that quickly disappeared. Dove jumped to her feet. "Whateva, I was only testin' you. Anyway I got shit to do, see ya'll later." Said Dove before leaving.

CHAPTER 15

Mad at the world for always setting Taylor up with the good ones, while she got stuck with the Bernard's of the world, Dove stood, wiped her mouth and glared at Cleotus. "Uh ahn nigga, I just sucked yo musty ass dill pickle. You gone give me a liter bottle or I swear I'll tear dis storage room up!" Dove shouted. "Shh!" Cleotus spat, then clamped a hand that smelled of sour milk and musty feet over her mouth. "Okay Dove damn. I was just joshin', I got it." Breathing heavy Dove dusted dirt off her knees and snorted. "Well don't josh wit' me, cause I ain't in tha damn mood." Cleotus nodded and hurriedly opened a box of Hen-dog, pulled out a liter bottle and smiled, showing off a fucked up grill. Uh! Nasty! Dat shit looked like he'd been chewin' bricks. Snatching her shit she stomped up front, grabbed a handle bag, two cups and two cans of Coke. Taylor's ass had her so damn mad she could spit fire. Sneakin' out the back, 'cause dese pitiful, beggin' ass mofos ain't need to know her business, she bumped right into Shelly almost droppin' her bag. "Bitch! Watch where da fuck you walkin'!" Snapped Dove. She thought about friskin' herself to make sure Shelly hadn't ganked her ass and remembered the only thing in her pocket was lint; which was the reason why she'd just sucked off Cleotus' ole perverted ass. "S..sorry." stammered Shelly. Eyes bucked wide, hands in the air like she was the po-po 'bout to take da pus'. With a snort, Dove eyed her ass up and down cause a micky flicky couldn't pay her enough to go there with her nasty ass. she might be a hoe, but she had morals, standards. With a roll of eyes Dove kept it pushin' and made her way over to Naugatuck Street, where a small park sat with six benches and a b-ball court. A game of two on two was already in progress when she copped a squat and winced when a sliver of wood from the bench slid up an asscheek. "Damnit!" Reaching down in her jeans, Dove quickly pulled it out, grimacin' at the blood coating the tip. Flicking it in weeds Hartford's Parks call grass, she resumed sitting, cracked the Hen-dog and filled the lil plastic cup more than halfway before poppin' the soda. "Ahh," dat Hen-dog's da truth." she thought until thoughts of Taylor intruded. Dove had always been the go to girl when it came to boys and men. It started with mom dukes having her sit on 'play' uncles laps, where she'd get candy and up to five bucks. She liked gettin' money, who doesn't, so she was all in. Idly watchin' the ball players, she heard Dave's annoyin' ass voice and zoomed in. Dave at one time had been a possible of hers. You know, its possible I'll give you some play cause you cute and keep a lil cash, but he fucked that shit up wit' dat lame ass dick game he had. Dove snorted, then squinted, wait a cock and balls minute, is that? Hell yeah, a pleased smirk slid on her lips. Kione. Ump, staring at an invitation Jarvis had just dropped off, my lips turned up in disbelief. Omaire's ass was straight retarded, dis fools invite read: Come join Omaire in a night of music as he releases his first single from his upcoming album 'Busta' (bitch u stank trick ass) perform- ing at Lou's nine p.m. on March 7, 2016. Word? More like, boy you suck, talentless ass. If Omaire wanted to be laughed off stage, hell yeah I'ma go and help that shit along. A quick bang at the door scared the shit outta my ass. "Who is it!" "Glenda. Taylor, open up girl." "Dis bitch." snatching open the door, Glenda bounced in all happy n shit. "Sup gurl, why you all bouncy n shit at eleven in the a.m?" Glenda continued bouncin', doing a combo of the pee pee dance and shadow boxin'. "Gurl you ain't been listenin' to tha radio?" "Nah, I'm watchin' Jerry, why sup?" That's the last time I'ma ask dis ding bat. "I entered dat contest to hit up da oldies R&B concert at Foxwoods Casino and I won!" She screamed, my eyes widened. I'd totally forgotten about the concert so busy runnin' between Ty and Omaire's demanding butt. Our once in a while thing had grown ever since he'd rolled up and Dove had tried to scoop. Now he'd call, pop up or send Jarvis every other day. A bitch ain't complainin' mind you, cause he looks out something lovely on the money and gifts tip; but sometimes I don't wanna be bothered, listenin' to all that damn s..s..s..stutterin'. "Oh yeah, whose performing?" "Blackstreet, Dru Hill, H-Town and my boo thang Keith Sweat, anndd, drum roll," she smacked her thighs, "I've got an extra ticket, wanna roll?" "Hell yeah, but won't yo girl Dove feel some type of way?" I asked, like I gave a fuck. Glenda gave a long tooth suck and flopped on my couch, my lips tightened. The switch jiggled cause dese hoes act like my shit came from Rent A Center or sumthin'. My shits real damn leather, not that pleatha crap. Broads needa learn when ghetto ass meets real top notch shit to sit like they got some damn class, fo' she catch a punch to da forehead. "I ain't feelin' Dove right now." Glenda grabbed my Newports, shook one free and lit up. My jaw dropped and the switch flipped on a lil bit. Hoes in Nelton Court know one thang if nothin' else, Taylor Janae James don't do nuthin' or give nuthin' for free; unless its benefittin' me down the line. "Glenda, I know you kinda slow wit' sum shit, but remember the words comin' at cha. Don't ever, never ever

ever, touch my shit without askin' first. I don't play dat hunny."
Glenda froze like dat dude from Batman was in the room, eyes
all wide n shit before finally noddin'. 'Sorry, I hear you Taylor.
It won't happen again. So I think Dove set me up with the Rich
incident." Arch of brow. 'How so?" Glenda crushed the cig
out, spillin' a lil bit of ashes on my Gemelli glass and steel coffee
table. That beauty costed over three big ones and I don't mean
hundreds. It looked like one round table, but opened into two
and dis chick gone spill ashes and not try and make an attempt
to clean it; Rememberin' how her shit looked like a spin off of
Sanford and Son. Aww shit, I'm showin' my age fuckin' wit'
Glenda the dumb witch of the north. 'Well she popped up in
the middle of the night a few days back, drunk as fuck mumblin'
a buncha nonsense 'bout how you a hater, be dick blockin' and
shit. Den she started flappin' 'bout she ain't know Rich was
gonna beat my ass like dat when she gave him my addie." Eyes
and mouth wide I stared speechless. 'So when she passed out I
went through her purse and guess what I found?" Finding my
voice, I squeaked out a, 'What?" 'Lindane and Acyclovir, it's to
treat crabs and herpes." 'Da fuck! I been lettin' dat hoe sit her
oozin', crab walkin' pussy on my damn toilet and furniture!"
Came out extra loud, not givin' a hoot who heard me. Oooh
wait til' I see dat bitch. I give two fucks (and we already know
how I feel about that) about Dove bein' shiesty, shady or wateva

until she steps to me. Dove can whine til' da hoe hoarse, but to know yo snap trap ain't right and happily flop yo ass on my shit, called for a beatdown. I froze. Aww hell naw! Dis trick had wanted me to put my face on her fucked up oozin', crab crawlin', open sores snatch! No wonder her shit smelled all foul, bitch smell so rank she make bathwater run, pus' so polluted she need to wear some Odor Eaters as a maxi pad. "Damn!" "I know. I don't have any proof that Dove told Rich it was me he got the shit from but while he was kickin' my ass he kept mutterin' "Mary got tested and came back wit dat shit." "Fuck, I need an appointment ASAP. Dat oozin' hoe been sittin' on my damn toilet." I snapped, switch all the way on. Glenda giggled. "Woosa Tay'. Unless you used it within five minutes of Dove, you should be fine." "And how tha fuck you know Dr. Glenda?" Again with a giggle. "'Cause I had crabs before, well more like six times, but anyway. The walk in clinic gave me a bunch of pamphlets on STD's and whatnot." Glenda stood and made her way to the door. "The show starts at nine. Think you can be ready, 'cause we'll be ridin' by limo?" she opened the door. "Lata, I gotta hit up the mall."

CHAPTER 16

I totally enjoyed my time with Kione's fine ass. Of course it would've been better if Dave got hit by a runaway bus, 'cause dude was a straight damn hater. Shit like, "Yo son I hit that." or "Her pussy need an overhaul, trust, yo boy on that shit.", kept pourin' out his loose ass lips. Til' Dove flipped the script and told Kione 'bout the time somebody (her) put Ipecac in his drink which shut down all chatter, 'cause he was to busy callin' earl. With a muttered curse, Dave strode off givin' them as much privacy as a park allowed in broad daylight. Kione was really interestin', not that she gave a shit about him bein' adopted and that he'd moved from Ohio to search for his real mother, like really? Fuck for!? She obviously gave his ass up for a damn reason. Maybe he should be thankful that he didn't wind up with a mother like hers. Dove did a bunch of bullshit noddin' like she really gave a bird's pussy, then made a quick move with the ole hand on the thigh move; only for his ass to grip her finger, lift her hand and place it back on the bench followed by a bunch of malarkey on how he was feelin' Taylor and didn't wanna fuck it up. Not that there's anythin' wrong with her he'd said; she was cute and all, he just wasn't interested. Bastard! Pissed off all over again Dove stomped from the park, Dave's laughter floating in her ears. Lookin' delicious in a purple Balenciaga dress and heels, hair done in loose curls, some jewelry, gloss and bam! Perfection at its finest. Glenda texted the limo was on its way, so I snapped a few selfies and threw 'em up on the Book and Gram so bitches could hate. Grabbed my purse and strutted to the door smellin' and lookin' fab-u-lous. And wouldn't you know it, there stood Rosalie. 'Bitch why yo ass at my door?" Steppin' fully out forced her broke ass to back it up, which was a good thang cause she smelled mustier den a mafucka. "The fuck!" I gasped, choking when the smell slid down my throat. 'Girl you stink, fuck you been doin'?" I backed up a few feet and told her, 'Stay there, I can hear you." Jeezus Mary and Joseph! Rosalie started cryin', spinnin' dis crazy tale on how Brick and her daughters had gotten into a scuffle when Toni came home and saw he and Kelly in bed. How Toni cried and shouted she was pregnant, only for Brick to force Kelly to beat the baby outta her sister; blah, blah, blah. 'Look Rosalie, dats all real tragic and all; especially since you knew they both were fuckin' Brick and you condoned it.

But I got somewhere to be." just as I said that a limo rolled up and out stepped Glenda lookin' like a whole new bitch. Fresh shoulder length reddish blonde sew in, bone straight with a part down the middle, while a grey and pink Nogara onepiece fit like a glove. My eyes dropped, Miu Miu stilettos with spiky heel, even her make-up was on point. Was a bitch in Oz, cause this broad done a whole three sixty on my ass. 'Come on gurl our rides here!" She yelled all loud like I was down the damn street, then hopped in the backseat and whooped. Bitches, I swear they see somethin' new and don't know how to act. Niggas right when they say you can't take a hoe out tha hood. Side steppin' stinky mcnasty I got my strut on, hips swayin', breasts bouncin'; knowin' all eyes were on moi, as they should be. Foxwoods stood on acres of land. It boasted everything from six casinos, diamond star hotels, restaurants, golf, theaters and retailers. As the limo rolled up I could see thousands of people arrivin' by car, cab, bus and limo; and all with a look of 'I'm gonna break the bank' looks in their eyes. Glenda was babblin' 'bout nothin' as we strolled through Foxwoods, takin' in the sounds, smells and people. 'Gurl, I'm fuckin' sexy ass Keith Sweat tonight." bragged Glenda as we reached the theater where a long ass line awaited. Luckily it was movin' fast, 'cause I would've went off ya heard. Some lanky mafucka took our tickets, nodded to some chick who led us in like we were at a Secret Service event and shit.

Glenda damn near skipped down the aisle when she realized we had front row seats. 'Ooo I can't wait!" gushed Glenda, eyes wide as fuck as she looked around, 'I should've worn a dress so I could've flashed Keith dis pretty ass snatch." I almost swallowed my damn tongue. I ain't wanna steal her joy, so I let her have that. The lights dimmed just as I peeped some lady walkin' around takin' drink orders. 'Foxwoods ya'll ready to partayy!" Yelled a voice, the crowd responded with a, 'hell yeah!" The lights flicked up on stage and there stood H-Town, minus one; older, but still sexy as fuck. Bitches started screamin' while the chick to my left started fannin' herself. 'Well...yeah...yeah!" Females lost there mind as the lyrics to H-Town's classic 'Knockin' Boots' began. Head boppin', I mouthed the words, eyes glued to Solomon 'Shazam's muscular ass as he pelvis thrust across the stage. 'Damn that buff nigga got my goodies wet." Glenda moaned like her ass was a blink away from cummin'. If so, Foxwoods better rip that mafuckin' seat up and replace it, I'm just sayin'. They finished to hella applause, then came Dru Hill. Ole gurl next to me ran up and tried to climb onstage, only for security to snatch her ass up and drag her up the aisle with a whole lotta cursin'. Chucklin' I peeked at Glenda who appeared star struck. Once they finished, the DJ re-appeared and announced a quick break. Since that dumb ass waitress never returned, I got up and made my way up the aisle to get a drink; so by the time Keith Sweat came onstage and Glenda cut up, which she surely would, I'd have a nice buzz goin'. Three different concession lines, one for beer which had a list of different brands, another for wines and the last for food. I normally ate when I knew I was gonna get right, but dese mofos done lost they minds wantin' ten bucks for a damn hotdog, twelve for a burger and that's without cheese, da fuck?! Jumpin' on the beer line, I was starin' at the selections slash prices when I felt someone starin'. Yeah I'ma bad bitch and get stared at on da reg, but dis shit was actually creepin' me out. The switch jiggled as my eyes scoped the scene and collided with a nice lookin' specimen of man meat. Red bottom kicks, black Escada jeans, John Varvatos cream button up and a nice sized diamond in the right lobe. Dark chocolate skin lay over a frame like Dwayne 'The Rock' Johnson, a bald shiny smooth head, chinky eyes and fluffy pussy eatin' lips. Hmm, my clit hardened. To his right, some chick was babblin' until she noticed his attention wasn't on her. Loud as it was, I could hear her snappin' on dude. Followin' his starin', she locked onto me like a homing pigeon, I smirked and gave a wink. Dude smiled, pearly whites blinding. I don't know what he told her, nor do I give two fucks. He started towards me. 'Sup beautiful?" he greeted, voice a la Michael

Clarke Duncan. God bless the dead wit' his sexy ass. I would've sucked dem balls down to da gristle, and tossed dat niggas salad, ump. "Aren't you gonna get in trouble with your watchdog?" His smile deepened. "Nah, ole girl knows to play her position." My brow arched. "And whats that?" "As my date for the evening, which will end if you say the word." Ooo dis big bastard was smooth, I'll give him that; and a knee to the nuts too if I wasted my time on his big ass and he was workin' with five. My smile dimmed at the thought. "Whats your name beautiful?" "It's gone if yo ass packin' five inches." I told his ass, no need in pussy footin' around; I'm just sayin'. A stunned look slid over his face. "Well damn shorty, tell me how you really feel." Steppin' closer, he grabbed my hand and pressed it against his crotch, his look intense. Hunny chile if dude thought I'd shrink back all embarrassed, his ass would be the one surprised. Smirk in place, uncaring about the crowd or his date Lassie, I reached in dem Escada's and let my fingers do the walkin' like his dick were the yellow pages. Hmm. His dick started hardenin', nice girth, he was circumsized, balls the size of medium eggs, his length maybe seven. Doable, and yeah I'm a dick conessiour. I can do that shit blindfolded, fresh outta a deep sleep and by lookin' at a photo, don't be J I'm just sayin'. "My name is Taylor." I withdrew my hand. "I'm Jake. Damn beautiful you got me wanting more." I rattled off my number just as Lassie approached. "Bay our orders ready its forty-five fifty." She said while eying my fineness up and down. "And you are?" Came out icy as fuck, I shivered then smirked. "Nice meeting you Jake." "Hold up." Jake went in his pocket, pulled out two fifties grabbed a pen off the counter and wrote his number on the edge. "Call me beautiful." Ole girl gritted like she was dying to take it there. Dat shit's hilarious 'cause if Lassie wants it, bring it so I could dog walk her beastly ass. All dat teeth knashin' and eye widenin' don't do shit ova here. "Thanks boo, I definitely will." Steppin' off, I decided fuck a drink. I'd eventually catch the waitress, 'cause if Lassie kept eyeballin' me, I'd be the next one being pulled up the aisle. No Diggity started playing, people were on there feet chantin' Blackstreet when bam! There they were, and juicy panties if Teddy didn't look finger lickin' good! I want to melt in your mouth, not in your hand, I'm just sayin'. I hated when Teddy's ass left the stage, but when 'I want Her' started with a lotta flashin' lights, Glenda started screamin'. Security selected a few a'ight bitches to go on stage and when he picked Glenda, she damn near knocked one girl down tryin' to get up there. That shit was funny as fuck. Keith walked out and Glenda jumped around like she'd won on the Price is Right, garnering quite a few looks from the other six on stage. He started pelvic thrustin' and that hoe burst into tears. I'm like damn, if its that serious let the nigga know your alive. Strip, whisper in his ear you'll suck his dick so good you'll suck him inside out, but all this extra crap was to much. He broke into 'Something Ain't Right' and like dis crazy hoe read my mind, she danced in front of him, reached out and palmed da dick. Muttered somethin' I couldn't hear, swept a leg out, took him to the floor and jumped atop his ass humpin' and hollerin' at the top of her lungs!

CHAPTER 17

"I'm just sayin' dat shit was fucked up." pouted Dove. I made her sit her ass on a plastic handle bag, no way I'm lettin' a bunch of crabs and whatnot rest on my shit. "Y'all could'a invited me to da concert. I like R&B too." she griped, sounding like Charlie Brown's teacher; I'm just sayin'. "Dove shut the fuck up. Whinin' and bitchin' about a concert six damn days ago makes no damn sense." "And whats up wit' dis plastic?" her ass cut in like grown folk weren't talkin'. The switch jiggled. Lorrdd please hold me back from drop kickin' this hoe and please make sure when she leaves she takes her company with her, amen. "Bitch you know why!" I snapped. Sorry lord, but Dove's ass is askin' for the switch to flip. "First of all hoe, I'm grown and can go and do who I want, when I want. Second, I don't need you nippin' at my damn heels everytime I make a move; and third, yo nasty bird, swine flue pussy havin' ass lucky I even let you park it on my sofa. Plastic or not, you just make damn sure you use every drop of cream and swallow every damn pill then hit up the clinic and get another dose, shot or whateva it is you need to get right. 'Cause you's a nasty, triflin' ass hoe and I ain't fo'got how you tried to play me at the hotel. Know yo boundaries bitch, fo' I really hurt up yo fuckin' feelings." Mouth agape, wide eyed, Dove stared like her ears deceived her. Knowin' how nasty she is, her shits probably full of dirt, wax, roach eggs and shit. I shuddered at the thought. She smirked. "Well damn, tell me how you really feel; and as far as STD's, don't act all pure and holy. I'm sure you've had your share, so climb off yo soapbox Oprah." Dove stood. "And for the record dumb ass, you can't catch anything from me sittin' here, fully clothed." Ooo, dis chick tryina bring it to me! In my shit no less! We stared at each other a moment before Dove laughed. "By the way, I hung out witcha boo Kione the other day. Did you know the nigga's adopted and here searchin' for his sorry mammie and that he finds me attractive? We're goin' out to dinner. I do believe that means you've lost yo shot, not every man wants yo ass Tay'. So take a step back and evaluate yo shit, hoe." Fuck it. Four quick steps and I was on that ass. Hello, may I take your order please? Yeah, let me get a six piece, two legs. I kicked dat big mouth skank in her kneecaps; two breasts, punched her in dem big ass nipples she called tits; and two backs, when her ass went down, two kicks to her back. Will that complete your order? Nah, let me get a Pepsi. I wrapped them newly done block braids round my fist and drug her ass to the door, banged her shit on the jamb; oh yeah add on an apple pie and finished with a kick to the jaw that rolled her right out the door. 'Listen up you hag fish smellin', big nipple havin', crab carryin', herpes sharin', jealous hoe. Don't do me boo, 'cause you don't want worse then what you just got served. Now take yo self on and when you learn to respect moi, maybe I'll let yo ass back in." I slammed my door and laughed. Teeth grinding, Dove stared at the bruises dotting her body. 'Fuckin' bitch snuck my ass, but its all good. You live and you learn right, and I'd learned that I needed to bring Ms. High and Mighty Taylor James to her knees. That ho needed to pay and I'm just the bitch to do it', thought Dove. Wincing a lil as she pulled her shirt down, Dove stared at the red mark on her jaw that looked like a sneaker sole. 'Ole brick foot bitch skank." she muttered, grabbed her Revlon make-up and got busy covering it up. 'Ooo I hate Taylor James mugly ass!" Dove screamed out, then stomped her feet a few times for good measure, which actually made her feel a lil better. Stepping over dirty clothes, her flip flop snapped when she stepped in a semi hardened mass of spilled grape Kool-Aid and apple jelly from the sandwich she'd made three nights back. Stuck, Dove snatched up her foot, only for her foot to rise and the flip flop stayed put. 'Damnit!" Kicking off the other, she bypassed overflowing smelly garbage, a sink full of dishes covered by roaches searching for scraps, a stove so grimy, greasy and dirty one would have to stare at the stove's sides to determine its orginial color and over to the fridge. Snatching open the door, she stared at a few slices of ham, two eggs, a six day- old quart of milk and a half eaten Chinese food. Flipping up the lid she gave it the sniff test and frowned at the sight of a pregnant roach giving birth atop pieces of pork, 'Goddamnit!" Tossing that nasty shit back in the fridge, she did a mental count on how much dough she had, while cursing Rich's dumb ass out for getting caught for Glenda's assault. The judge slammed his ass with two years in jail and two of probation upon release. 'Fuckin' loser." Shaking out pink and white Jordans, she made her way outside and ran smack into Omar. 'Ow!" Slid out. Colliding with a bag of bones hurt like a mafucka. 'Fuck Omar watch where the hell you goin'!" Rubbing an aching tit, Dove gave him the screw face. 'Sorry yo. Where yo ass in a rush to?" Asked Omar, givin' Dove the eye. 'You all soft n shit, let a nigga part them thighs girl." 'Damn, you blunt wit' it." Omar licked his lips. 'Why fart around when I see somethin' I want. I let it be known." Dove smiled, feeling good 'covered in bruises and still pullin'. Fuck outta here Taylor, you ain't got shit on me boo,' 'Oh yeah, and what would happen if I did?" Purred past parted lips, she slowly gave 'em a lick. 'Sheeit, actions speak louder than words." drawled Omar, then licked his chops in return. Suddenly Omar was lookin' kinda right. Omar wasn't very tall, maybe five six and was a high yellow color with piercing black eyes. He kept his hair in five cornrows braided to the back and always wore oversized white tees and Levi jeans, Jordans on his feet. 'Please," Dove snorted, then damn near choked on a wad of phlegm. 'higga you gotta come betta than offerin' up a wet ass." Enlightment brightened his eyes. Before she could blink good, ninety bucks waved before her broke ass eyes. With six dollars and fifty cents in her pocket, two bucks on her foodstamp card, (she sold the four hundred as soon as it hit on the first) that ninety was lookin' damn good to her ass. A quick look around, then Dove snatched his behind back in the crib, slammed the door and ignored the disgusted look he made no attempt to hide. 'Strip." 'Right here?" Omar stupidly asked. Dove nodded. Although her living room could use a good cleanin', her bedroom looked much worse. She wanted some dick and she wanted some more of that cash Omar carried, so living room it was. 'Yeah fool, right here. Hell, if you can get it poppin' outside, this should be a piece of cake." Dove swiped a bunch of clothes and a half box of Tampons to the floor, pulled off her skirt and thong; and glared at Omar. 'Are we gonna do this or not? 'Cause I got shit to do." 'Uh..hell yeah." Omar grabbed his tee, yanked it over his head and Dove gasped in surprise. Ole Omar wasn't scrawny like I'd thought. Instead he had a nice frame, pecs, sexy grooved six pack and muscular arms. Her eyes lowered waiting to see the rest of Mr. Omar, and when he dropped jeans and boxers her jaw literally dropped; what had to be ten fat inches sprung free. No lie her mouth watered, her kegals clenched and her asshole puckered. "Gotdamn Omar." Dove quickly wiped drool, pulled off her shirt so damn fast her side twinged, and jumped on the couch; threw one leg up on the couch's back and the other on the three legged coffee table. Omar gasped at the beyond extra hairy pus' before him; pus' so hairy he could make a wig. Shit so thick he could make mittens at least three pair. With a shrug Omar almost slipped on a lone sock, then kneeled between silky thighs and gave a deep inhale. Kinda tart was his thought before divin' in with long tongue strokes. Dove laid back enjoyin' the feelin' that swept over her as that tongue swirled, twirled and feasted so damn good her ass had lifted off the couch in pleasure. "Shit! Eat dat pussy Omar, eat it! Uhh!" Orgasm brewin', curlin' up toes as it slid up tensin' calves and quiverin' thighs, when he suddenly started gaggin'. Her eyes popped open, only to see Omar gaggin' and wheezin'. A clump of wet, goggy, pubic hair flew out and plopped on the table. They stared at each other, neither saying a damn word, next thing she knew her whole body shook and tensed when that big bastard of a dick shoved inside. "Shitt!" she hissed out as Omar fed ten inches up her intestines by the time balls slapped ass. Gruntin', Omar started strokin'. 'Now I'm an honest bitch." thought Dove. 'Yeah I've been around the block, but that monster took some gettin' used to; and the way he worked it had me cummin' back to back in no time." 'Don't cum in me boy, I ain't on tha pill." Omar kept right on goin', sweat beadin' his forehead. He gave one powerful thrust and she felt sperm coat her insides, then he spat, 'Mornin' after pill." Her eyes widened, not cause of that hot shit he'd just said, but cause his dick was still hard. That chocolate mafucka glistened with combined juices, makin' her mouth water. 'Umm, let me getta taste." Omar did as told. Grabbin' that monster she noticed he was uncircumsized; nasty, but no biggie. Openin' wide, she slid in as much as she could without gaggin' which was nine, tongue swirlin' all around suckin' up every drop. 'Smelly pussy or not, her juices tasted awesome and niggas thought so too' because they stayed dinin' on these snacks. Wait a minute, what the fuck..." Dove ran her tongue around the rim and felt a bump. At first she was like okay, its probably a hairbump; but when she twirled it around again and felt at least six, "Tha fuck?" thought Dove. One last suck and Dove yanked it free, examinining like she had a magnifying glass in hand. Ignorin' cries of why'd you stop, Dove grilled that boner in dim lightin' cause she hadn't opened the blinds and gasped in shock. Six medium sized bumps that looked fulla pus stared back at her, wet and shiny with saliva. Her eyes snapped up, 'Fuck is this!?" Came loudly flyin' out. Omar cleared the slick look off his face so fast she wondered if she'd really seen it. 'Bumps, fuck you mean?" Omar snatched his dick back and slid on his boxers. 'I know that smart guy. Why you got 'em and what are they from Omar?" Dove asked again her throat suddenly felt hot and acidity. 'Girl you trippin'. Yo ass wasn't worried it when I was beatin' dem guts, now it's a problem? Hoe, I ate dat smelly ass pus' and ain't nan question." Dove jumped up, hands on hips, eyes glarin'. 'Nigga, a lil smell never killed nobody. Can yo rocky road dick say the same!" Omar sucked his teeth, slid into Jordans, then tossed four hundreds atop the coffee table. 'Fuck outta here yo, my dicks my business. I hitchu off, we can do it again or not, peace." The door closed behind him with a soft snicker. 'Wow, you did all this for me?" I asked Kione. He'd invited me over where he'd prepared steaks, baked potatoes and a chef salad; followed by blueberry cheesecake. 'Yep, I wanna show you that I'm not just interested in getting you into bed. I'm interested in the whole package." My face heated. 'Aww, how sweet. I'm feelin' you too Kione and honestly it kinda scares me." Kione took my hand and gently kissed it. 'Don't be, I won't hurt you Taylor. Give it a chance, give us a chance." Smilin', I leaned in and kissed Kione; my thong immediately soaked. 'Umm, why don't we skip dinner and get right to dessert?" I huskily whispered. Scooped up the cheesecake and with a sultry sway of hips, started down the hall and into Kione's bedroom. Once there I only paid attention to his king sized bed. Setting the cheesecake atop his bedside table, I turned, kicked off my shoes and slowly wound my hips while shimming from shorts, then cami top. Proudly standin' before Kione in dark blue and white bra and matchin' boy shorts. I winked. "That's right boo," I thought. "Drink all dis fineness in. I'm a stallion boo." Turnin', I jiggled butt cheeks then sat on the beds edge and gave the c'mere finger move. Kione divested himself of clothin' revealin' a muscular frame stacked with tattoos. My eyes greedily bounced around, settlin' on tented boxers. Oh yeah shits on now! R. Kelly's 'Twelve Play' began playin'. "Aw yeah, this lil nigglet had some game." He picked up my foot and started kissin', nibblin' and suckin' the digits and a bitch almost flew off the bed. No nucca had ever done that shit before! Got diggity damn, momma done found her a freak a leek! Thank you Lord, thank you jeezus and all his decifils, amen! Kione trailed kisses up my legs, then bit my mound through my boy shorts. My legs parted like the Red Sea as juices leaked down the crack of my ass in anticipation. Kione inhaled and groaned. "Damn, you smell good." Usin' teeth he pulled my shorts down. That was cute and all but enough teasin', I wanted the dick right damn now. So I hit the front clasp enclosure, relasin' firm juicy mounds and succulent nipples, hard and ready to be pleased. I gave 'em a squeeze and gasped when tongue met clit. I came all on that mug, squirtin' what felt like gallons. Kione smacked, slurped up every drop then did somethin' with that Godlike appendage that had my ass seein' stars, moons and clovers. Shruggin' out of boxers, nine curved inches came into full view as he slid on a condom. 'Sss, unh dat feels so good." I purred and threw my legs up on strong shoulders. "Fuck." grunted Kione as the bed rocked and my eyes rolled. Kione rolled and I found myself on top, my favorite position. Grindin', buckin', hips swivelin', a bitch went to work. No way I'd let young meat turn me out and have my ass lookin' fo' him wit' a flashlight. The name is Taylor, not Glenda or Dove, smank you! Within minutes I had that shit and when I spun around reverse cowgirl it was a wrap. Ooo dat lil nigglet did my pussy right goddamnit! Just thinkin' 'bout it got da snacks meowin'! Anyway, I'm at Chilli's havin' lunch wit' Jake, the youngin' I met at Foxwoods and babe, in good lightin' his fine body should've been somewhere earnin' top dollar as a model. I bit back a yawn, cause I had a late night, plus dis nucca was runnin' down his complete bio, like I gave two shits. I'd rather hear if yo dick shootin' sperm like a speedin' bullet, I'm just sayin'. Born in Windsor, bussed out to Simsbury, first girlfriend at fourteen, ha! Got dat cherry popped at fifteen, never been arrested, didn't have kids, had a condo, drove a Lex and worked as a personal trainer to the well off out in Haddam. Oh my God my pussy dryin' up listenin' to all dis crap! 'So where's your side kick? She ain't gonna come outta nowhere is she?" Jake choked on his slushie. 'Oh..well..she's probably at work and that ain't my damn side kick. She's just a friend, why, you scared or sumthin'?" I burst out laughin'. 'Is dis nucca serious? Scurred? Moi? Obviously he don't know who he's talkin' to, cause tha only thang I'm scurred of is not being able to handle tha dick, to swallow dat motha, slurp up his balls and lick da ass at the same damn time. Shiittt ask bout me boo!" A few patrons looked our way. 'Scurred? Me?" I pointed a freshly done fingernail at myself. 'Hunny, you got da wrong female if that's what you think. Taylor ain't neva scurred, not of a bitch or tha dick." Jake smiled, reached across salads and took my hand. 'And I can't wait to find out. I'm packin' and so far I ain't neva met a chick that can handle what I'm bringin' to the table." My clit convulsed. 'Oh yeah, well let's be out. I can eat at Chilli's anytime." Sheeit, Taylor James neva eva passes up the chance to twirl on some peter. Good thing I got my Summers Eve on this mornin'! Vinegar does a bat cave good, I'm just sayin'.

CHAPTER 18

"Gurl I'm tellin' you, Taylor's bad news." said Rosalie while smackin' on salted cashews to Glenda. They both sat outside gossipin' and watchin' noonday traffic strollin' past, on foot and in cars. "Why you bein' such a hater Rosalie, I thought ya'll were cool?" Rosalie snorted. "As cool as one can be with a cobra. Taylor's out for self, you'll see that soon enough." Glenda stared at Rosalie and wondered again what had happened between the two. True they'd never hung out, but Rosalie hadn't knocked on Taylor's door to beg and borrow in months. Instead her ass was comin' to her place all throughout the day, sometimes so early she'd wake her from a sound sleep for somethin' as asinine as a cup of sugar. "Blah, blah, blah, I didn't know its bash Taylor day. If that's all I'm gonna hear, I can go find some balls to lick, fo' real." Rosalie's eyes widened. "Well excuse me for bein' concerned and tryina open yo blinders." snapped Rosalie. 'Ah uhn! I know beggin' Benny ain't tryina bring it to me, not when her own weeds were growin' outta control." thought Glenda. Lips tight, she grilled Rosalie for a hot second, then smacked her lips. 'Whateva girl, tell it to Taylor since you all up her donkey worse than an ass injection." Popping another handful, Glenda peeped Brick roll up with Kelly and Toni who each swapped spit with him before steppin' from the car. 'Well batwings and syrup, what'ya got here!" Contemplated Glenda with wide surprised eyes. 'Well, well, why you ain't share dat nugget of gossip; since you sharin' everythin' else? Ooo is yo ass fuckin' Brick too?! Ooo dat jungle bunny must swing a baseball bat to wrap up two sistas and dey momma." laughed Glenda. Rosalie looked pissed, so she must've hit tha pussy on tha clit, as Tay' would spit, I'm just sayin'! 'Hmp." clacked Rosalie. 'I ain't Taylor." she stressed the latter. 'I'm not out here suckin' and fuckin' every dick in sight. I have standards and would never do such a disgustin' thing." she spat all righteous and shit. 'Now I know I'ma lil slow when it comes to processin' stuff, but a tramp ain't stupid okay. People try and play me as such and sometimes I let 'em, that way I can hear everythin', cause nuccas and hoes have no fuckin' filter. Example: Omar's ass runnin round fuckin' and getting' his dick wet while carryin' syphilis and HPV, which is genital warts. His body was a walkin' smorgasbord of infectious diseases." thought Glenda. 'How do I know? His ex girl Brenda had been a virgin and after datin' two years, most spent listenin' to Omar bitch and gripe about havin' blue balls; Brenda finally caved and gave Omar the snacks. Only to go in for her yearly gyn check up and find out she was not only preggers, but also a walkin' cryin', snotty mess of diseases too. Brenda tearfully told Janet, Omar's mom who in turn told the world. That old trick can't hold water once liquor, beer, wine coolers touched them big ass black lips." mused Glenda. 'As sure as I get a check faithfully every month, ole Rosalie was fulla shit.' 'Hey ma." greeted her daughters. 'Don't hey ma me. I told ya'll to clean up before leavin', y'all bounce and leave tha place a fuckin' mess. I'm yo mother not yo maid." Kelly sucked her teeth then pulled a long strand of hair off her tongue, gross! 'Damn girl, check yo teeth before leavin' the motel, young, dumb and fulla dick hairs." thought Glenda with a silent giggle. 'Whateva ma." snapped Toni, still feelin' some type of way after damn near getting' lock jaw from continuous suckin' of Brick and three of his boys. He'd given her four hundred lousy dollars while his precious Kelly got her loose pussy eaten', got to ride Brick's pole and handed two g's with a trip to New York this weekend for new gear. So hearin' mom dukes bitch about a mess no doubt made by she and her creep thang Jacko wasn't her concern. 'Please, we all know you and hairy back Jacko got ya'll freak on. House probably smells like a beached whale. Dem dishes from you tryina show Jacko yo stove skills, which you don't have, so if anyone needs to be cleanin', its yo fat, lazy ass." and with that Toni stormed inside. Mouth agape, Glenda stared, waitin' on Rosalie to jump on her back for the disrespect, and ride her in the house while poundin' the back of that melon she called a head. Not! Rosalie just sat there crunchin' on cashews. 'Ump, I wish my son would!' thought Glenda. Speakin' of Marvin, she whipped out her cell to give his daddy a call to see what day and time he was droppin' him off. Kelly took a squat on the stoop, Glenda swore she smelt eggs n cheese. She dunked her hand in the paper bag for a handful of cashews. 'Guess I'm done, cause if her canal smelled like boiled eggs n cheese imagine what dem fingers do.' "Terrance residence, Grace Terrance speaking." said Marvin's prim, proper and up tight wife. Glenda hated her ass for a number of reasons, but Marvin marrying that halfwit when he'd never asked her, stuck in her craw sumthin' serious! She'd been with Marvin from the age of twelve til twenty-two with no break ups. She did what she had to to help pay his way through medical school and what thanks did she get? Marvin breakin' up with her before the ink dried on the M.D. after his name; goin' behind her back and getting' primary custody of there son and then marrying that chick outta nowhere. 'Hello? Is anyone there?" Brought her back to the here and now. 'Yeah, where's Marvin?" Snapped Glenda through clenched teeth, Grace sighed all dramatic and shit. Glenda knew she was rollin' her eyes which made her smile. 'Marvin is at the office, did you try him there?" 'Now see, her ass knew she was forbidden to step foot inside his precious office and all his staff knew not to put her calls through', ole prissy ass. 'Well put me on hold, call his ass and find out what time he's bringin' my son home." stressed Glenda, 'cause Grace's womb was useless when it came to holdin' a baby. Marvin had spent crazy dough tryina fix her rotten shit; Glenda laughed aloud at the thought. 'Sure, hold please.", was that smugness she heard. 'She gone make me read her stupid ass.' vented Glenda. Some opera type music played in her ear makin' her feel like she was on an elevator, bitch. A click and her annoyin' voice was back. Truthfully she'd rather listen to the corny music that had been playin'. 'Marvin said his last patient's at five, he'll drop Jr. upon completion. Anything else?" Teeth grindin' so hard, Glenda thought she'd cracked a molar; she hung up on that skank. 'Aww, lil man's coming for the summer?" asked Rosalie big smile on her face. 'Yep." Glenda cheesed, then stood, 'I'm gonna make somethin' to eat." 'Ooo whatchu makin'?" both Kelly and Rosalie simantanesouly said. Surprise colored her face. "Huh?" Greedy eyes didn't blink. "You said you 'bout to cook, what? 'Cause a bitch ribs scratchin' her back." Rosalie threw out "And whats that got to do with me? My name ain't Bricks or Jacko and I don't own Save-A-Lot." then flounced inside.

CHAPTER 19

Man I was on a roll! Dudes were comin' at ya girl left, right and center; but that's what a chick of my caliber handles on the daily. Between seein' Ty, Omaire, Kione and Jake my body needed a break, so I made a spa appointment and invited Dove since we hadn't hung out in awhile. She agreed to meet me over at Chan's Day Spa. Those Chinese mofos were ghetto as fuck, but they could do some work! Chan's was located on the Berlin Turnpike, which was full of everythin' one could think of. A superstore Wal-Mart, Target, Hoffman's Gun store and a chain of fast food eateries to name a few. When I arrived Dove was seated in the waitin' area, flippin' through a People magazine; dressed in a cloth, red, mid thigh hoodie dress. The material reminded me of a bath towel. "Heyy girl." greeted Dove, eyes runnin' over my frame. If she was searchin' for flaws she'd be searchin' all damn day, cause moi is always flawless. Chen, one of the owner's appeared, head boppin' to the loud sounds of Shaggy's 'Boom Boom'. His black jean shorts saggin' on his thin frame, a Chinese symbolled medallion swayin' with every step and a pair of Ray Bans rested atop a bleached blond Mohawk. 'Ah my favorite customer has arrived!" He yelled, Dove chuckled. This was her first time at Chan's so if she thought Chen was funny, wait until she met the rest. The bell over the door chimed announcin' the arrival of more customers. 'Ho!" Screamed Chen and Dove's face twisted, arms akimbo she glared and spat, 'Uh ahn, I know you ain't callin' me no hoe you chinky eyed bastard!" Chen rolled his neck. 'Chill home skillet. Chen no call you Ho, me call brother. But why so angry, you don't like bein' called what you are?" I burst out laughin' as Dove stood mouth gapin' wide. 'See, you in position to catch big dick." Her mouth snapped shut just as Ho appeared, wearin' what looked like a karate outfit minus the belt; his shoulder length salt and pepper locks pulled back in a ponytail. 'Ho, shouhui." Ho nodded, waved and headed down a hall littered with family photos, flowers and pictures of there homeland. From what I saw I wouldn't mind vistin' and latchin' onto one of those smart, rich ones. I might not've spoken Chinese, but I know what I needed to; shit like number two, General Tso's and pork fried rice, I'm just sayin'. Anyhoo, Ho led us to a changin' room and disappeared. Colorful lockers, comfy chairs and couches and beautiful thick robes and slippers with Chen's imprinted on both. 'I was 'bout to go off. You know I don't play that disrespectful shit." huffed Dove. Honestly I'd only caught half of what she'd said, Dove was full of shit. If I remember correctly, my cousin China pounded her shit out at Glenda's, so she needed to chill on all that rah rah crap. 'Hello, my name is Fa Li, please come with me." said this curvy chick with a heavily made up face. 'Bout time." muttered Dove. Dis tramp gone set off tha switch if she don't chill. Lips smackin', signalin' Dove she'd jiggled the switch and she needed to chill, we followed Fa into a big room with two massage masseuse, whateva tables; a row of oils, lotions and aromatherapy scented candles. I even spotted some acupuncture needles. 'Would you like refreshments?" Dove grinned. 'Hell yeah, Fa Lee hook us up." 'Stupid, it's Li, not Lee like Bruce." Dove shrugged. 'So, anyway gurl, what we gettin'?" Takin' a deep breath I walked over to a small stereo and CD selection, chose Mariah and Mary J's 'Whats The 411'. Dove's ass was fiddlin' with the needles, fucked around and stuck herself and started bitchin'. Switch all the way up I served her ass. 'Listen, I'm tryina be nice and show yo ass sumthin' different, how I get down with keepin' my shit tight; but yo ghetto ass up in here actin' a fool. Cussin' out staff, touchin' shit.... sit yo ass down, shut the fuck up or get dressed and bounce." Eyes wide Dove silently assessed to see if I was serious, best believe hell yeah I am. 'Jeez, sorryyy." Dove took a seat, Fa returned carryin' a tray with two fruity drinks, brown sugar smokies, marinated grilled shrimp and bacon stuffed mushrooms. "That's what I'm...I mean thank you, it looks delish." said Dove. "Your welcome. Chen says you are getting the works, I will start you off with massage and facial. You pick out scent you like and tell me if you want man or woman to see you half naked." "Man." "Woman." we said. Fa nodded, the door opened and in walked a buff dude wearin' cream linen pants, wifebeater and bamboo flip flops. I quickly made my selection, untied my robe and got on the table, reached for a stuffed mushroom and sighed in bliss. "This is Keung, he will massage friend, Ji will be right in." Half an hour later, I was so relaxed I could've melted and slid off the table. From there it was facials, then pedi and Mani's. The eight hundred-dollar price tag was well worth it. "Mmm." Damn Ty's tongue was a mafuckin' beast! I know I said I was takin' a break, but fuck dat, dick and dollas call, best believe I'ma answer, I'm just sayin'. "Shit." I moaned as that snakelike appendage had my asshole puckered, then swept down, teasin' clit; fuckin' catchin' every drop that rained down, slurp! That's right boo, get all them minerals and vitamins. Hips swivelin', I pinched hard nipples sendin' me right over the edge. Breathless, sweatin' I collapsed face down, then gasped anew when hot hard dick opened me up. Ump, ump, ump, Ty was doin' me right gotdamnit! Pussy juices rained down saturatin' sheets and probably the mattress too. The headboard rapped out a beat as I threw it back. "Yes Ty! Yes! Harder boo, tear dis gushy up!" And he did. Slammin', long strokes, jabs, hips pistonin', reachin' down I teased my button hard clit feelin' another orgasm approachin' fast. "Uhn." Legs weak and shakin' like I'd suffered a seizure, Ty reached over on the table, snatched up a fat blunt and lit up. My nose wrinkled. "Eww, fuck you smokin'? That shit smells horrible." Ty picked up his voice box, placed it against his neck and said, "Loud and fanta." "Hunh, how you smokin' orange soda? I swear, ya'll mofos will smoke and snort any damn thing." Ty chuckled, at least I think he was. "Nah shorty, fanta is a tobacco leaf. You put it in with your weed, I like mines crushed so I can sprinkle it evenly. It's also called grabba." "Oh." Best believe I got my smoke on, but I ain't neva heard of this grabba and the way it smelled I'd keep on not knowin', thank you. An hour later I was in the kitchen buck naked whippin' up smothered pork chops, homemade mash potatoes and cheesecake when I turned around and saw a jewelry box atop the table; and Ty with a serious look plastered on his face. "Open it." I damn near skipped to the table, flipped up the lid, peeped the ring inside and cheesed. A five carat canary yellow diamond bling with ruby baguettes winked back at me. "Fuck me." I whispered, then swallowed back drool. "Glad you like it. Will you marry me Taylor?" Ooo fuck me the long way and thrice on Sunday. 'Um..well..' 'Don't answer now, just wear it and think about it. I can make you happy Taylor if you give me a chance, anything you want is yours." Damn! First, didn't dis nucca know I'm already married; and second, even if I wasn't no way on God's green earth would I ever do that stupid shit. 'Okay." I heard myself say. 'I'll wear it and think about it." After that hot crap I had no appetite, so mumblin' what I know not, I got dressed and hauled ass from Ty's place like I had wings on my heels. High as hell I laid across my couch, thoughts of my previous life circlin' like vultures over a fresh kill... It had been l-o-v-e, longing over visiting erection at first sight when I saw Mason's sexy self. Six three, caramel, his cut up frame covered in tats, sexy almond shaped hazel eyes, just walkin' perfection at its sexiest. Within weeks we were a couple, he was twenty-one, I was fourteen. Age didn't matter and neither did what my parents had to say, so they kicked my young ass out. No problem, I moved in with my boo Mason. We partied, fucked, partied, drank..... hell, I even rode around with Mason when he did his dirt. Sure I had run ins with other broads Mason dug out, but I was numero uno and defended my status as such. When I hit fifteen, Mason traded in drug dealin' for robberies; drug dealers, check cashings, it didn't matter. If Mason wanted it, he was gonna get it and he wanted to rob an armored truck when they pulled up at Webster Bank. Things were goin' good accordin' to one of Mason's partners in crime, this dude named Nugget, until Hex, his other partner tripped. His gun went off, catchin' one of the guards right between the eyes. Return gunfire escalated, somehow Nugget and Mason got away. Hex, who'd been shot twice, wasn't so lucky. After surgery he was handcuffed to his hospital bed. Mason and Nugget made off with one million big ones which they split down the middle. Leavin' everythin' behind we hit the road. Mason was smart, he hid the majority of the cash in his grandmother's backyard, beneath an orange tree. We thought we were good when we safely made it to the Big Apple. Mason had family in Manhattan so that's where we went, unaware that Hex was awake and singin' worse than a parakeet. I'd just found out I was pregnant and when I told Mason he was over the moon. We went to city hall and got married and when Mason slid on a black diamond ring I didn't even know he had, I burst into tears of pure joy. Of course we had no way of knowin' his supposed cousin Diamond had heard about the robbery, shootout and fifty thousand-dollar reward. Diamond happily made the call that would send my hubby away and with Hex claimin' Mas was the mastermind. Mason was quickly sentenced to forty-five to life. Mason told me to raise his son and to go on without him; he wouldn't call, returned all my letters and refused my visits. Eight months later I delivered the son he proclaimed I'd have. I was fifteen, scared, lonely; so I did what I felt best, I gave him up for adoption. Which is why I hate hospitals, it reminds me of what I'd given up years ago. "Well, well, well. I thought you'd never call." Purred Dove while jumpin' for joy. Omaire had finally got some act right and called up the right one Dove Mitchell, not tired ass used up pus' Taylor'. Omaire chuckled. "I d..didn't forget..t you. I've b..been busy." "Oh yeah, with what?" 'Hopefully his ass said out buyin' my new wardrobe for when I strolled on his arm.' thought Dove. "T..T..Tonight I'm p..performing at Club Lou's." Eyeroll. 'Jeezus Mary and Joseph spit it out already!' "Are you invitin' me?" coyly slid out. "Of c..course, v..vip all the w..way." "I'll be there and maybe after your performance you and I can have a lil privacy so I can show you my appreciation for the invite." "W.. word?" "No doubt, I'll see you tonight." Omaire gave the info then ended the call. Smiling wide, Dove did a fist pump, then raced to her closest, she needed to pull out all her tricks. Sittin' in the hair salon, Dove eagerly listened to salon gossip when talk turned to Taylor. Ears burnin' tryina catch every bit, she leaned a lil closer. "Ain't dat trick like a hundred." said one girl gettin' rollers put in. "Who cares? She's a man stealin' skank gurl." said another gettin' a perm. "Hmm, you know she messin' wit' Ty too." Dove almost choked on her Sprite. "I ain't surprised. Trampy spreadin' dat old twat around to anyone willin', but when she messed wit' mines that calls for a beatdown." Perm head nodded and smacked thick lips. "I know that's right. She needs a lesson in 'keep yo dick beaters off' fo' real." "Yep and as soon as I see her its on, Jake is my man. I worked too damn hard to get where I am to let some old bat take mines." "Yeah, she's one fake bitch." Dove threw in her ten cents. "Do we know you?" Rollers asked with a whole buncha eyerollin'. I smiled. "Nope, but we share the same enemy. Taylor's grimy ass done smiled in my face while fuckin' my men." lied Dove. "Men?" A nod. "Yep, she stole my man of five years. I'm like fuck it, he wasn't mines if she could snatch him. Then I got another man and I stop by her house and my new man answers the door. So if I can help her ass get whats comin', I'm all in." smiles broke out. "Tell us more..."

CHAPTER 20

Lou's was packed, cars sparklin' from car washes lined up; Lex's, Beemers, Audi's and more. Their occupants spillin' out in there best finery, Armani, Bottega to name a few. A photographer's bulb flashed bouncin' off jewelry causin' a dazzlin' display for those hidden in the darkness; hungry, waitin' for the opportunity to collect every goodie in sight. Inside highly glossed floors and staff eager to take coats and minks for a tip. A horse shoe shaped bar was busy makin' drinks for thirsty patrons, while the smokin' section burst at the seams as expensive cigar smells mingled with cigarettes and Black & Mild's. Omaire was hyped as he watched the turn out from inside the office, a half dozen monitors showed inside and out. Dressed to impress in a handmade original by his ex Tamisha, Omaire knew tonight would be the start of big things. He planned on bein' bigger than his father ever was, he'd show everyone he had what it took to be a rapper. Dove stepped up in

Lou's lookin' like a true diva wearing a metallic number by Nogara she planned on returning first thing in the morning, and a pair of Miu Miu's she'd borrowed from Taylor's closet. Stridin' to her seat, eyes on swivel for Taylor and the two chicks from the salon named Marion and Jennifer. Ump, dozens of cuties were in attendance, most with bitches on there arms which didn't faze her, 'cause she'd walk right up and shoot hers; punk didn't course through her veins. Omaire had Jarvis scoop me up for his big night and I definitely had jaws droppin' in my black and tan Lee Yau cut out one shouldered dress, and Max Azria's on my cute pedicured feet. My hair was in an updo with a bang swooped to the side and Chanel diamonds Omaire gifted me with blinged in my ears. Bein' shown where to sit, I was pleasantly surprised to see I had front row status, until I peeped two things, Dove's salty ass four rows back and Omaire's parents with his busted ass aunt Doris six seats down from me. My fist balled and eyes narrowed. Well, Well, Well, as long as grumpy and stinky stayed in their lane I'd be cool, but no doubt the switch would jiggle if I caught her ass starin'. The lights dimmed and out walked loud ass Jenny Boom Boom from Hot 93.7. I'd never met her, but she annoyed me just the same. I tuned her out, choosin' instead to people watch. Damn, so many dicks to ride, whats a girl to do? I need to make up some cards and pass dem shits out, hmm, but what to say; 'Wanna dyk suck? You've tried tha rest, now cum to tha best, or how 'bout, 'Love to gobble dyk and balls if you got more than a snack, hit me up, I'm just sayin'. That sista group Cherish took to the stage singin' the three hits they had, two of 'em had gained some weight and was sweatin' up a storm. Hell, her ass looked like she needed a bottle of Gatoraid, a towel and a damn break, I'm just sayin'. These chicks looked desperate; desperate for a comeback, desperate for a loose fittin' outfit, just f'n pitiful. Chuckle. Dude to my left tapped my hand. "Excuse me, I don't know if you're here alone but I need to tell you, you are absolutely beautiful. My name is Dr. Joshua Browne and I'd love to take you to Italy for dinner whenever you'd permit me." My brow arched. Well that was new, Italy hunh? A small smile graced my lips. "I'm Taylor, nice to meet you." Joshua beamed, revealin' deep dimples and extra white choppers. Joshua lightly caressed my knuckles. Hmm, I hadn't done white meat since ole Brandon, who by the way was still callin' and textin'. I'm like damn dog, if I don't answer yo calls and ignore yo texts, buy a fuckin' clue. As I always say, it's gotta be sumthin' in it for me; unless I'm doin' a lil charity work, I'm just sayin'. "I betchu say that to all women." I silkily purred, then winked. Ole Josh wasn't bad lookin', in fact, he gave some black men a run. Even sittin' I could tell he hit the six-foot mark. He had olive toned skin, thick slightly wavy locks, broad forehead, thick brows, extremely long lashes, greenish blue eyes, aquiline nosed, kissable lips beneath which rested a goatee. He wore a Balenciaga double breasted tan suit which coincidentally matched my dress perfectly; and on his feet, Brian Atwood loafers. His wrist held an I. Gorman diamond faced watch. Nice. Real nice. "How do I know you're not an ax murderer?" I flirted with a flutter of lashes. "Never that. I like my woman alive, so, will you allow me that pleasure?" Joshua reached into an inside pocket on his suit jacket and withdrew a card; it read: Joshua B. Browne M.D. and above it, Brown and Sikes Pediatrics, specializing in premature infants. My eyes widened. Dude's for real! At least a normal Joe wouldn't spend cash on a good stock of cards with raised fancy lettering. "I will definitely call you." I uttered just as Omaire took to the stage. "Hello club L..Lou's!" He yelled over the mic. Joshua nodded and turned back towards the stage, leavin' me to wonder how Omaire knew Joshua since he was kid free. Applause rang out as Omaire started rappin', my eyes shot wide the fuck open, dis ninja wasn't stutterin'! What da fuck!? Did he take some 'how not to stutter classes?' A nice ass beat, sorta like Busta's 'Whoo Haa' came on and Omaire blared, "Ho I buy you diamonds, ho I bought you pearls, what chu thought, bitch you stank trick ass, when we go out you eyeing otha niggas, phone hotline ringin', bitch you stank trick ass..." Not bad, I've heard worse from some of these so called rappers today. Omaire rapped two more songs, one of them a slow, love ballad titled, 'Cum on My Tongue'. Now that joint I was feelin'. Omaire took a quick break, so I stood intendin' on makin' a bathroom stop and grabbin' a drink from the bar; unaware that Dove had found her flunkies and pointed me out. Dodgin' through heavy foot traffic, I finally made it to the back and down a hall where two men and ladies restrooms awaited. "Taylor! Wait up!" yelled a female voice I didn't recogonize. Turnin' I observed two chicks walkin' in my direction. One was tall as fuck for a woman, at least six three with banana yellow skin covered in freckles; while the other, once she drew closer, I realized was Jake's date from the oldies R&B concert. "Dis bitch." my lip curled like I smelled shit on a shoe. "Do I know ya'll?" Tall girl rolled beady eyes and smacked glossy lips. The switch jiggled. "Please," spat Jake's date. "Don't act like you don't know who I am." "I don't." I simply stated, I knew her ass was steamin' mad which tickled me to no end. "Girl quit talkin' and punch dat homewrecker!" People gave quick glances before continuing along to the restrooms. "Stay away from Jake, I won't warn you again." she snarled; feelin' big and bad cause she had Sasquatch with her. "And if I don't?" Givin' a fake shiver like a bitch was scurred the switch flipped up and a smirk slid across my face. "Listen lil girl, I'ma grown ass woman. I fuck who I want, when I want and you and big bitch ain't gonna stop my show. Maybe if you up yo sex game, we wouldn't be talkin'." "Ah uhn Clover, you gone let her talk to you like dat?! Couldn't be me, I'd jump all in her shit!" She snapped, so much bass in her voice I had to check the throat for the ole Adams apple. 'She-man shut tha fuck up. Matter fact, why you here and so concerned 'bout her mans dick? What, you ridin' it too?" 'Slut!" Clover roared and swung. I saw that shit comin' a mile away, blocked and served Clover with one to the eye. She staggered, but I still caught her with another to the jaw, just not as hard as I would've liked. 'Fuckin' bitch!" yelled She-man. I thought he-she would swing, instead she came down on my foot with all her weight. 'Oww!" Hoppin' on one foot I punched he-she's tall ass in the gut and when she folded expellin' tart breath. A knee caught her in the face, nose bones crunched, blood shot out, followed by a piercin' scream. Before I could finish he-she off, Clover jumped on my back. Foot achin' sumthin' serious, I refused to go down. Bein' beaten by Clover wasn't happenin'. Grabbin' a handful of hair that felt hella greasy, I flipped her ass over my shoulder. Clover's body hit the floor with a loud thud. Joshua suddenly appeared and snatched up Bigfoot, givin' me opportunity to beat fire outta Clover until security arrived and snatched me so hard by the arm my joint felt dislocated. 'Mafucka!" Kickin' back I caught dem eggs, scrambled 'em and his ass crumbled to his knees with a whole buncha groanin' and gaggin'. More security ran up and wouldn't you know it, the only black guard tackles my ass like he was goin' for a pass or whateva the fuck they do in football. Pandemonium broke out as those who'd witnessed the altercation all spoke at once, tryin' to explain that I'd been protectin' myself. You damn right, I wasn't the aggressor, at least not at first. Joshua walked up and ordered. "Let her go or you'll be standing in the unemployment line. Those two are the ones you should be manhandling." the crowd shouted in agreement. Catchin' dudes name, Robert as he helped me up, I noticed Dove leanin' against the wall, look of disgust on her face. Ooo so my supposed girl saw the whole shebang and didn't help a bitch? Ok...filin' a mental note, I winced when shoulder and foot throbbed. "Are you alright?" Joshua asked concern alit in sexy greenish blue eyes. "I'm okay, I think." "Here, let me help you." Joshua scooped me up amid much oohing and aahing. I could feel Dove, Clover and She-man throwin' much hate my way, so I smiled through the pain, wrapped arms around his neck and milked it. Chapter 21 Oh my God, did dis trick have a good luck charm? Did she luck up on a fuckin' genie to grant her ass three wishes?! Here she is sleepin' with half of Hartofrd, luckin' up on dude's wit' dough and two stupid broads couldn't take her down, wtf! Teeth grindin', Dove sat over Glenda's tossin' back Yak, smokin' up her bogie's and ventin'. Yeah, Yeah, Dove knew Glenda's behind couldn't hold water and she'd run and tell everythin' said; but Dove didn't care ya heard. She was done, fed the fuck up out chere. There had to be a way to bring Ms. High and Mighty down a peg, or two; fuck it the whole damn ladder. 'Damn gurl, slow down fo' yo ass fall out drunk somewhere and get robbed and raped." Dove arched a brow in disbelief. 'Hoe don't be tryina throw no jinx on me with bein' robbed." spat Dove half slurrin'. Glenda chuckled. 'Girl I can't with you. Anyway, whats good with you and that stutterin' rapper and handicapped man goin'?" Blurry eyed she stared at Glenda tryina determine if she was fishin' to report back to Taylor or really interested. 'Fuck all that, whose layin' the pipe to yo backed up cootch?" Gaspin', Glenda stared. 'Hunh?" 'Ump. If you can hunh, you can hear. Shit you all up in mines but don't wanna share who been knockin' down cobwebs." Glenda gave a sneaky look around. 'I'm like really, who da hell she lookin' fo'? Far as I know its just us out here.' thought Dove. 'Welll," drawled Glenda. 'I've been creepin' wit' Marcus and sometimes Brick." 'Brick!" Dove yelled shocked as shit. 'Damn, Brick can a bitch get a slice, 'cause I heard ole boy carryin' round an anaconda in dem boxers'. 'Shh. Damn Dove, tell the whole project why don't chu." she snapped jumpin' to her feet. 'Please, I wish her ass would, I'll stomp her ass so good she won't know up from down,' contemplated Dove. 'And how long you been dick jumpin' Ms. Thang?" Glenda smiled all dreamy and shit, would her ass still be smilin' if Okra suddenly found out? 'Long with Marcus. As a matter of fact, Marcus and I would've been together if I hadn't caught him comin' outta Rosalie's one night and when I confronted him he admitted he'd been bangin' Rosalie. And Brick, we've sexed maybe six times." her voice lowered. 'I let him bag up here and things just happened." 'Well damn, maybe I need to offer up my place so I can get a lil sumthin' sumthin'. 'I hope you getting' more than a lil dick for him usin' yo place Glenda." 'Ain't nuttin' lil 'bout dat monster he's packin'." 'Well excuse the hell outta me." Glenda giggled. 'Besides it ain't that serious, Marcus and I spend more time together. Now don't change the subject." 'Mommy I'm hungry." said a lil kid who walked from the back. 'Marvin go make yourself a sandwich and grab a glass of milk." 'Can I have chips too, please?" Glenda nodded. 'Aww snap, I ain't know lil M was here. He done got big." 'Yeah he came Wednesday; and yeah he's eight now." Lil M, which is what I called Marvin Jr., definitely did not favor his father. Marvin was crispy black, while Glenda was more toasted almond; Lil M was damn near light bright white. Where Marvin Sr. was borderline anoxeric, lil M was chunky. I could go on but it was obvious, even to the blind, that lil M wasn't his. And since Glenda got around, she most likely didn't know who it was. Hmm, interestin'. 'Anyway gurl yeah, I gets mines but I ain't got one special man. I got my eye on a few possibles, but I haven't nailed it down yet. It's Friday, plenty of dick down at club Twenty-One, wanna go with?" Lil

M walked past chip bag hangin' from his teeth, glass of milk in one hand, sandwich in the other. "I'on girl, lil Marvin's here." "So, he ain't no toddler. Leave his ass right here with instructions not to open the door for anyone. We'll sit a couple hours then come home." Glenda fidgeted, eyes sweepin' back and forth as if an answer would leap from the walls. "O..Okay, I'm down. What time?" I smiled. "Eleven be ready." "Did y..you like t..t..the show?" Asked a hype Omaire. After beatin' dem skanks down, Omair whisked me away to his home; grillin' me on what had happened that almost ruined his breakout performance. 'Please.' I silently snorted. 'Breakout hunh? The only breakin' goin' on was me poundin' bitches faces.' I'ma pro boo, I do what it do and handle mines. Be it curlin' a mofos toes or smackin' a hoe. I'm like the mail, I deliver pussy, head and beatdowns; rain, sleet or snow, ask 'bout me bitches. Leanin' over on the couch to the sounds of Maxwell, I unzipped Omaire's pants, reached inside and pulled out my Cracker Jack prize. You know, sweet n nutty, yum! Openin' wide, my tongue snaked around while inhalin' Omaire's scent of Tone soap and musk. That shit got my nipples hard. And just as I knew he would, Omaire halted all complainin' and started moanin', followed by ass liftin' from couch. Smirkin', I took him deeper relaxin' throat muscles, nose met pubic hairs. "Sss." hissed Omaire, eyes rollin' in pleasure. "F..Fuck T..Taylor!" I drew back, releasin' with a loud poppin' sound, Omaire hurriedly shoved slacks and boxers to his ankles and smiled. Quickly standin' I shed clothin', pulled a condom from my bra before removin' it, then thong. Stuck the condom wrapper in my mouth, kneeled and resumed suckin' while unwrappin' condom, removin' and slidin' on a dick hard as steel. Dats right, fuck tyin' a cherry stem in a knot, getcho game up, learn from me hoes. I left Omaire's ass snorin', slobbin' and droolin'. His snores kinda sounded like his stutterin' he'd start, stop, then sputter and start anew. Helpin' myself to four g's, I called for Jarvis and had him drop me over Kione's since he'd texted while I was busy. Kione lived all the way up Blue Hills on the Hartford, Bloomfield line in a cute single family yellow house with detached garage. I'd been by once but hadn't paid his place any attention, so I found myself scopin' everythin' from immaculate grass to meticulate paint on the trimmin'. Stridin' up the walkway a voice called out, 'I know yo ass ain't goin' to see my man." Startled, I looked around and finally saw some chick standin' on the porch of what looked like a house that a stiff wind would blow over. 'Excuse me?" Maybe she wasn't talkin' to me, could be a cellphone or bluetooth around, so I gave ole girl benefit of the doubt. Until she stepped off a loudly groanin' porch, wearin' dirty ass bunny slippers. Flicked a cig in calf high weeds and crossed the street. 'I said I know you ain't goin' to see Kione." she spat, beer fumes peltin' me all in my damn face.

Now I like beer as much as the next bitch, just not by the keg, I'm just sayin'. "And who the hell are you to be askin' me my damn business?" Ole gurl laughed revealin' one missin' front tooth while the other was an ugly brown, like she'd rubbed shit on her tooth and let it harden. Face wrinkled in disgust, I gave her a quick once over. Bunny slippers, her heels ashy and dry as fuck. Shit so dry I could strike a match; so ashy I could flour a buncha chicken. Knock kneed, stained jean shorts that looked like they were chokin' her snatch, a pink tee she'd tied in a knot to show off a flat belly with a navel so damn big it looked like a ten year-old's thumb. Shoulder length reddish blonde hair that hung in a snarly mass, her face was a'ight, I guess. "Cause I'm his side chick. If Kione needs a lil release I'm right here, willing and able to handle anything he desires. So you can hop back in yo ride and beat it, bitch." The switch jiggled. "Why don't we let Kione decide." Reachin' out to ring the bell, I was thrawted by dis chick grabbin' my wrist with her nasty ass paws. "We don't need to let Kione decide jack doo doo squat, you heard." I socked her ass dead in the mouth. Her ass screamed like I was killin' her, so I gave her sumthin' to scream about when I punched her twice in the eye. "Trick, you don't know me! Long as you ashy don't eva step to me!" I yelled, unaware of Kione who'd flung open his door upon hearin' the commotion step outside. "Aww snap! Is dat Taylor!? Yo son she beatin' da brakes offa Shae Shae!"

Damn, even though I was focused on whoopin' tail, I'd recognize that voice anywhere. Fuck was Dave doin' ova here? It was eleven thirty, shouldn't his ass be somewhere trickin' fo' da pussy? 'Oh my God! Kione help me!" cried Shae Shae, who was now on Kione's nice lawn takin' kicks from head to toe. 'Yo Dave, don't just stand there, help me man." barked Kione. 'Sheeitt, I'm tryina see sum tits. Hold upa sec." declared Dave eyes wide in anticipation. 'Yo!" 'Okay, okay, don't bust a vessel. You da man Kione, can I be like you when I grow up?" Dave joked. Kione grabbed me, leavin' Dave to help busted ass Shae Shae to her feet. 'She attacked me! Trick you lucky Dave's holding me back." I stood there smirkin' when Dave quickly let her ass go, threw up his hands and stated, 'Hell go for yours ma. Never let it be said ole Dave kept you from bein' stomped out." Shae Shae rolled her eyes. 'Fuck outta here. Dat hoe snuck me, just like she snuck ova here to fuck mines." Kione burst out laughing. 'What? Go head wit dat dumb shit yo." I giggled at the past pissed look upon Shae Shae's face. 'I know you ain't gone stand here and try and play me Kione." she snapped. 'Especially not for dis broad." 'Ma!" yelled a pre teen from across the street. 'Stone in here cryin'!" Shae Shae rolled her eyes. 'Well slap yo tit in his mouf til' I get there!" She yelled back. 'Eww dats gross he's my brotha. Besides, dis titty milks for Harmonica." My jaw dropped, what in tha rachet ghetto hell had I walked into?! Dis

193

Shae Shae chick was tellin' her daughter to breast feed her baby brother! I done heard it all! 'Oh so you gone act like I ain't been suckin' you and yo sidekick off everytime you call?" Kione chuckled. 'Shae listen....you listenin'?" She nodded. 'Yeah, I let you suck me off a few times, but as I recall you sucked off all ten of my boys too and everytime Dave's here. Yeah I call cause its him that likes the freaky shit you into, so don't stand here perpertratin' its more than it'll ever be." Shae Shae choked. 'Ah uhn, don't come fo' me Kione. You cute and all..." 'Girl shut up, lets go inside while yo daughter Ecstasy feeds her brother. I'll give you a golden shower. I'll fart in yo mouth if you suck me off first." said Dave. The fuck, I think I just threw up in my mouth, too much fuckery was goin' on with ole nasty mcnasty. Kione turned to me. 'Please come inside Taylor. I'm glad you stopped by and trust when I tell you this will never happen again." He pleaded puppy dog look on his face. Aww how sweet, he's beggin', sit, roll over, bark, I'm just playin'. Just to make tramp stamp mad, I gave Kione a big ole juicy kiss. His arms encircled me, then rested on my ass while that juicy steak between his legs stiffened and poked me above my navel. 'Mmm." purred out like a kitten bein' scratched. I could clearly hear teeth suckin' before Shae Shae angrily stated, 'C'mon nigga, I gotta get back to my son; and you will hit me off with a twenty and a bag of loud." Before stompin' inside.

CHAPTER 22

"Thanks for the invite." Dove lied to Omaire. His s..stutterin' self hadn't invited her, she'd called him earlier just to see what he was up to and to do a lil butterin' on how good he'd performed. But when she heard a bunch of commotion and asked what was up, only to be told it was a bbq/pool party Dove invited herself. So there she was lookin' scrumptious, feelin' good as Omaire's eyes ran over alla dis encased in a polka dot bikini; ready to strut and claim whats hers since Taylor hadn't made an entrance. 'Hopefully her Ren and Stempy ass wouldn't show.' was her thought. Omaire's backyard stretched for miles and was full of peeps; some fully dressed, others in trunks, bikini's and onepieces. Three huge grills wafted the scents of ribs, steaks, and more through the air, while servers took drink orders. "Y..you look n..nice." he stammered, smiling wide. "Thanks, so whats the occasion?" His smile broadened. "I got s..signed!" With a happy squeal Dove jumped in Omaire's arms, covering his face with kisses. "Omaire, I truly hope the young lady you're swapping spit with isn't the whore who punched me, you can do so much..." Dove turned and came face to forehead with Omaire's aunt Doris, she wanted to head butt her for interrupting. "Oh..I'm sorry, please continue. Wait a minute." her busy eyebrow rose. "Wasn't this young lady at the dinner as well?" Omaire nodded, but kept his arms around Dove. "I like her Omaire, hold on to her." Doris winked and strode off. "M.. mingle, eat, drink, I'll b..b..be right back." he made to leave until Dove grabbed his hand. "Where you goin'?" "To c..change, m.. meet you a..at the pool." Turning, Omaire strode towards his mansion her eyes following him every step of the way. Ooo chile there were all kinda delicasies at Omaire's pool; young and firm to old with saggy balls. Dove personally didn't discount the elderly like Tay's ass, 'cause they need to get off too. Just 'cause you smell like Ben Gay and mothballs, yo chest hairs grey and you've got more hair on yo back then head, don't mean jack if money's involved. A few chicks eyed Dove, so when Lady Saw's classic "If Him Lef" came blarin' through big ass club speakers, she twerked it, then jumped in the pool purposely splashin' broads stylin' in lounge chairs thinkin' they to cute to get wet. Not! Comin' up for air, Dove was face to face with scrawny, hairy, bird legs. Her eyes zoomed up and onto a package stuffed inside a mans bikini, up a hairy gorilla like frame and onto a face only a mother could love. then again, maybe not. Protruding jaw with tiny Chiclet size teeth, mis-matched lips, a pug nose and beady eyes, one of which roamed around in the socket. "Well hello there gorgeous." Dove wanted to laugh in his face but knew from Omaire's dinner, looks were deceivin', so who ever he was guaranteed he had dough. Omaire hadn't returned, so Dove went for hers. Smiling bright she stood givin' an eyeful of water runnin' down succulent breasts and hard nipples. Dude licked his chops, damn near droolin'. "And who might you be gorgeous? I've never seen you at Omaire's function before." "Dove and I'ma newcomer; and you are?" His smile grew. "Johnny Rae, owner of Johnny Rae's oil rigs." Her eyes shot open in surprise, oh snap! The Ojay's 'For The Love Of Money' started playin' in her head. "Nice to meet you Johnny Rae." "Same here." Johnny helped Dove from the pool, suggested they get a drink and talk, so with a nod Dove agreed, forgetting all about Omaire's ass. An hour later Dove's mouth hung open in shock, turns out this party was one big orgie! Mofos were getting' it smackin' everywhere! In the pool, on the deck, in front of the bar, a couple were even atop the speaker. People were swappin' partners quicker then she could blink, bottoms soaked and not from pool water, Dove drooled at the sight. 'Fuck it.' thought Dove right before reachin' out and yankin' down dat skin tight bikini bottom and gasped at the sight of what had to be a foot longer! Pre-cum oozed from the tip, makin' her mouth water. Opening wide, Dove sunk to her knees, her jaw cracked and popped as she took on the challenge, unaware that Omaire had three cameras rollin'. Kione was out like a light, snorin' damn near soakin' his pillow wit' drool as I padded barefoot to the kitchen for a drink. Flippin' on the light I snatched open the fridge, searchin' for sumthin' good to quench my thirst when somethin' fell off the front fridge door. Grabbin' a can of Sunkist I looked down and spotted a fridge magnet and a piece of paper. I guess when I yanked the door open I somehow knocked paper and magnet free. Poppin' the soda I chugged half, burped, then bent and scooped both from the floor. Placin' it back, the name atop the paper grabbed my attention, Maris and John Attorney at Law. Hmm, was Kione comin' into some cash? A quick look over my shoulder showed I was still alone, so I quickly got to readin'. We have located your birth certificate. (please see enclosed) I zoomed in on other papers attached to the fridge, but saw nothin' but notes and shit like, 'buy tires', or 'groceries' so I read a lil further. So far we have located your father who currently resides in prison, (call Sally if you'd like his prison information) your mother was born and raised in Hartford, CT we will continue searching and will notify you upon further findings. Tha fuck! Stomach swirlin', numb legs had me racin' to the livin' room where I quickly jumped into clothin' I'd earlier shed while watchin' the Untouchables with Kione. Could it be? Racin' outside, I took off on winged feet needin' to be home where I can focus, concentrate and find out if I'd been fuckin' my son. By the time eleven rolled around I'd drank a pint of Paul and was still a ball of nerves. Under my bed lay a locked mini chest that I kept all my important shit in, I kept the key inside the kitchen junk drawer. Both sat before me and yet I couldn't bring myself to open it. Maybe another drink would help. I tossed dat shit back and didn't even feel the burn. Takin' a deep breath I opened the box, pulled out the contents I sought. Pulled papers from a manila envelope with shaky hands and read what I knew by heart, I could quote word for word verbatim backwards and forwards. Tears flowed, throat burnin', I stared at the birth certificate, adoption papers and a name and phone number. Karen Booker, Mason's grandmother. I hadn't heard from, nor called Karen in years, twenty-six to be exact. There was no need to, I'd done what I felt was right and gone on with my life. "Hello." Shit. I needed to sober up 'cause I don't even remember dialin'. "Hello" she said again. Willin' frozen cords to work, I finally got out. "Aunt Boobie, can I speak to Karen? It's me, Taylor."

CHAPTER 23

Got damn Texas was hot as fuckkk! Sweat pooled under Dove's arms and trickled down her back, under her waistband and down ass crack. Nasty! Not even two minutes in the sun and she felt as if she'd darkened three shades from walkin' from the airport and again to Johnny's huge ranch style home. Horses and cows grazed lush grass and she could hear a couple chickens squakin'. 'I hope dis country boy don't think I came all the way here to milk cows and pick eggs. The dick good, but not that damn good. I'm made for shoppin', fuckin', travelin' and more fuckin'.' Thought Dove. "Nice place, but I hope you have AC cause I'm roastin'," "Sure, sure, anything you need lil lady; just let me know." Broad smile in place, Dove stepped inside and gasped. Exquisite furniture she knew had to be imported, blessed cold air assaulted her as her eyes jumped from Clive Metcalfe's 'Jaquar Cruising' to a free bird sculpture. Yeah a bitch knows a lil sumthin', I dated Webster Covington before he made it big. I dumped his ass 'cause I thought he'd never make it; too bad I didn't hang in there. 'Oh well, there's always ole Johnny Rae.' her thoughts continued. After showing Dove around, his maid prepared a lunch of grilled chicken cutlet with Middle Eastern spice rub, baby greens and bacon stuffed mushrooms. She had a Remy on ice with a splash of soda; Johnny Rae, a snifter of Courvoisier. Next thing she knew her vision was blurry and the floor rushed up to greet her... Dove didn't know how long she was asleep but when she woke some chick was all in her face like she'd never seen black skin before. Raisin' an arm that felt weighted down, Dove pushed her ass back and slowly sat up amid feelin' nauseaous and swirlin' ceilin'. 'Ugh." smackin' dry lips, she slowly gave a look around. A huge room, bare walls and at least two dozen beds, partially covered with breast high partitions and flowered curtain. 'Good, your awake. How do you feel?" Said the pale creature who'd been in her face. 'Fuck the pleasantries, where tha hell am I?" Ole girl smiled, revealin' two bottom teeth missin'. She burst out laughing. 'Ha, ha, ain't you in the wrong profession trick." Her smile fell. 'Well, at least I ain't the only one." she waved an arm, pointin' out the beds. Dove's eyes shot fully open lookin' over the room again. Now she could hear sexual moans and skin smackin' skin. 'In case your still in denial, you're in a whore house honey." she stood. 'We're locked in during business. Every girl here has a nightly quota, you meet your quota you eat....you don't, your punished. On weekends if you did good during the week, you're allowed outside....any questions?" "Any questions? Any questions! Hell yeah! Like where the fuck am I? Who the hell are you!? And where's Johnny Rae 'cause I don't belong here with you people!" The girls lips curled like Dove insulted her. "Yeah, yeah, I've heard it all before. Follow the rules, you'll be fine. Aas far as Johnny Rae, you'll see him soon enough to ask all the questions you like. And my name is Joy." Joy strode to the door, knocked twice, waited, then knocked once again. The door opened giving a brief glimpse of some wiry white guy that looked like a ferret, before it closed, then re-locked. Storming over to a window Dove made to lift it and make an exit when she noticed it was not only nailed shut, but bars blocked it on the outside. "Do you mind." a raspy voice snidely asked. Turning, Dove saw a pretty ass chick who looked around nineteen and of mixed decent. "What?" She rolled her eyes. "I said do you mind. I'm with a client and your interrupting." Dove looked but didn't see anyone in bed with her, all she saw was a laptop. Closer inspection showed an equally naked chick on screen, who she could hear moaning while three pussy juiced fingers slid in and out. "Oh.. sorry." Turning, she speed walked to the door and started banging. Fuck a signal she wanted out, right damn now! "How'd it go?" I asked Omaire who whipped out a usb and handed it over. 'B..better than e..expected, s..s..she hooked u..up with J..Johnny Rae T..Taylor." I burst out laughin'. That's what Dove's ass got. I knew she went behind my back and was tryina get with Omaire, who by the way told me everythin'. See, Omaire and I had history. I knew he was bi-sexual, hell, sometimes I picked up his sex partner for the evenin'. In other words, I kept my mouth closed, as long as when I asked for whatever, I got it. Omaire's parties were legendary because any and everything went, I even suggested Omaire have a yearly fee for admittance. I pushed play and watched Dove and Johnny havin' sex. I'll admit, dude was definitely hangin' and from the grimace and squeals comin' from Dove, whose pussy was loose and wide, he knew what he was doin'. Hmp, shit so loosie goosie Dove could fit a purse and pair of heels when shopliftin' and walk away normal, I'm just sayin'. So yeah, I asked Omaire for help. Why, cause that big mouf trout knew my secret I'd told her on a drunk night when the shit was weighin' me down. Anyway her ass stepped to Kione in the park and put a bug in his ear about his dear ole mom livin' in Hartford and if he got a lawyer in no time he'd be reunited. Plus she did Glenda dirty, she was cool peeps and didn't deserved dat shit. That bitch knew and didn't pull my card. That ain't no friend or associate, that's an enemy who needs to be taught a damn lesson. Johnny would let Dove go once I made the call, but until I did, he was to get his money's worth. "You need to tell him Taylor." said Glenda as we sat inside Applebee's havin' lunch. Sippin' on a Sex on the beach and smackin' on delicious appetizers; smoked trout crostine with radish and dill cream, inside out brownie bites, buffalo wings and more, to name a few. Glenda and Marcus were officially togetha, though Okra constantly harassed 'em both. I told Glenda to grab her cast iron skillet, pop her ass one good time and she'd leave 'em be. "I o'nt know." she shrugged. "I don't wanna be arrested 'cause I drew first blood by usin' a fryin' pan. And don't try and change the subject." Glenda lightly rapped my knuckles, the switch jiggled. Oh no she didn't hit me with the fork she'd been puttin' in her dick suckin' mouth. Grabbin' a wet wipe packet, I tore it open, pulled it free and wiped my hands with Glenda watchin' my every move like I gave a rat's ass about her feelings. Shit, I loved dick; the look, the smell, the taste, the flavor of cum slidin' down my throat. but here's were we differ. I brush, gargle, floss and visit the dentist, plus I'm selective on who can have these lips wrapped around their shaft. If it smells, has any bumps, oozin' anythin' other then pre-cum I'm out; no matta how much dough was involved. Whereas Glenda was like Dove, she just ain't give a hoot. I remember one time her ass was caught suckin' off Viktor behind the package store. Everybody and they momma knew Viktor's dick was covered in pus bumps that would pop and ooze blood and shit through boxers and jeans, gross! Only reason I let Glenda hang was cause I took her ass to the clinic and sat right there when he gave her her results. 'I know and I will. I just don't know how and what to say." Glenda smiled, picked up her Hi-C punch and said, 'Just be truthful. I'm sure Kione will understand why you did what you felt you had to do." stated Glenda. She stood up, 'I've gotta hit the lil girls room, think about what I've said." I watched Glenda weave her way through the tables full of dining patrons, my thoughts all over the place. I know Glenda's right, I need to step up; but the thought of what I'd done, we'd done, turned my innards. Yes I got around. Yes I've slept with a few associates sons, but I would never willingly sleep with my own child. Did I deserve what I was currently goin' through? Fuck no. And fuck anyone who thought so wit' a baseball bat. Glenda returned all smiles n giggles. 'What's up, peein' gave you a nut?" 'No silly. Marcus met me for a quickie in the bathroom." she wiggled her brows. 'Ooo you go witcho freaky self." I teased. 'So how lil M feel 'bout Marcus bein' around?" 'He likes Marcus, they go shoot hoops everyday. Last weekend we went to the carnival out in Windsor. He got him an Xbox One and a slew of games, then they play until I make them call it a night." 'A slew? Fuck is a slew?" I laughed. Our waitress walked up, asked if we needed anythin' else before leavin' the bill inside a leather binder. Twenty-seven ninety five. Pullin' my wallet out, I froze at the sight of baby Kione starin' back at me. I normally didn't carry this wallet 'cause I'd fuck around and lose my mind if it were stolen for that very reason. Yankin' out two twenties, I slid it inside, finished my drink and said, 'C'mon, lets do a lil music shoppin' over at Best Buy."

CHAPTER 24

Three fuckin' weeks. Three fuckin' weeks of bein' jumped by eight hoes 'cause I refused to gap my legs so someone could make money of her; of goin' hungry so long she'd drink faucet water and eat balls of toilet paper, then finally caved and fucked, sucked and even ate smelly pussies. She lost count after fourteen. Johnny Rae finally made an appearance, he and some lanky long dick black man tossed her around like a rag doll. Her pussy was so sore she had to walk wide legged. Her asshole throbbed so bad her eyes watered, shit, even her jaw fuckin' hurt. She tried everything to get away and all she got were slaps, punches and kicks, so Dove decided fuck it. She'd be the best hoe, she'd be top earner, earn their trust and make her escape and once she did, Dove Mitchell would become the madam and her first recruit would be Taylor. "Taylor this is a nice surprise." greeted Kione. I'd finally gathered my courage and popped up at his place. A look at crusty feets house showed the porch was empty which was a good thang, cause I'd douse her ass in water and watch her melt with the way I'm feelin'. 'Yeah, uh, hi. C..can I come in, or is this a bad time?" Please let dis nigglet say nows a bad time, lord. I know I neva call on you, but I am now. Give ya gurl a sign here. 'Sure." Kione opened the door fully. 'Sure, c'mon in." Damnit! Steppin' in I didn't see or hear that lil weasel Dave. Any other time his annoyin' ass was around and now when I need interference he's nowhere in sight. Figures. Takin' a calmin' breath, I steped fully inside to the smell of curry goat cookin'. 'Would you like a drink?" 'Fuck yeah!' 'Sure, I'll take a wine cooler if you have any." Kione nodded, strode into his kitchen and returned seconds later with requested cooler in hand. 'So whats up?" He asked again. I'm like damn nigga, don't rush me, shit. 'I" deep breath. 'I wanted to talk to you about you bein' adopted." 'Okay, what'd you wanna know?" 'Everythin'." So Kione started tellin' me his story but as I'm lookin' at him all I see is Mason, why had I never noticed that before? "...so I came here to find her." I zoomed in and heard. 'I believe I'm your mother Kione." blurted out, tense shoulder relaxed, silence loomed. Kione gave a broad smile. 'I know." 'Wait..what?!' 'Come again." 'I said I know. I've known before I met you at the cookout. Then once I saw you I knew, plus Dove told me you could be. Sorry it took you so long to figure it out." My jaw would've hit the floor if it weren't attached. "What?" I couldn't have heard that shit right. I couldn't have heard this ninja sittin' here all smug n shit, tell me he purposely had sex with the woman who'd birthed him. The switch flipped. "You ignorant ass mafucka!" Jumpin' up I glared in disgust at Kione. "Why? Cause I chose to keep quiet and fuck you?" He smirked. "The pussies on point by the way." Ooo he wants me to chop his ass one good time, its obvious aunty Boobie and Karen didn't tighten up upside his head. "Kione somethin' is seriously wrong with you, I see that now. So what was the plan? Get me to fall for you? Aannt! Wrong! Taylor doesn't fall boo, niggas d; which you've obviously done too." Bam! I smiled "Is mommy on point? Does yo heart race when you hear my voice? I betcho dick hard as bricks right now. Too bad, so sad. You'll neva ever see it, smell it, or anythin' else where dis twats concerned." A wicked smile slid across my lips at the look of anger on his. "So now what mom?" "Nothin'. You found me and extracted your so called revenge, now we're done. Any chance we had of bein' mother and son you'll find on that condom you flushed." I strode to the door, swung it open and walked out. Good riddance, bastard. Groggy as hell, Dove forced her blurry eyes open, gave a look around and sat up so fast she fell off her bed. Her bed! She was home! How? When? Last thing she recalled was eatin' dinner with a bunch of tired lookin' bitches. She kissed the mattress, the wall, danced out her bedroom and appreciated everythin' she looked upon. "Yes!" Fist pumpin' she flounced on the couch and kicked heels in joy. Yeah home, now its time to put her plan into action; payback would be sweet. She might not be able to prove that Taylor had anythin' to do with it, but her gut said she had. Soon that bitch would regret ever doin' her dirty.

THE END

SNEEK PEEK
COUGER 2

CHAPTER 1

A bitch was chillaxin'. I'd stopped by Ty's last night and as soon as I unlocked my front door, Jarvis was rollin' up. Got damn! Tha pretty, popular and sexy are always in demand, that be me bitches! Not really in tha mood, 'cause Ty wore a sista out, I gave him a call, lied and said I had cramps, then screamed in horror. "Oh hell naw!" Somebody had come in my shit and tossed blue paint all ova my damn furniture! Eyes wide in disbelief, I stepped back out, peeped who was outside, then walked inside. "Ooo I'ma kick some tail today and whoever did dis grimy shit better have some dough cause they're gonna pay for all new shit. Believe dat!" * Daylight hit and I was outside wearin' jeans, a tee and tightly laced timbs. No Vaseline required, cause I neva ever let a jealous hoe get close enough to scratch me. No way you gone have me lookin' an ugly mess, I'm just sayin'. Seemed like everyone and they momma was outside, like they knew shit was 'bout to pop off. And it was. The Courts held a lotta hatin' hoes which ain't stop jack ova here, cause I'ma fuck who I want, go where I want and say what I want. I'm just sayin'. Spottin' Kelly and dis chick named Mavis, I stomped over, adrenaline pumpin'; ready to take it to dis fake hoe once and for all. Soon as I get close, I peep tha sneaky look on her face. My eyes drop and there it was; blue paint under nails and a few splatters on knuckles. I o'nt know why dese youngins' get to smellin' they self and wanna come for moi, but her ass gone learn today that Taylor James don't play with kids. I get their asses sucked out at the abortion clinic, slurpp! I'm just sayin'. Runnin' up, I punched Kelly dead in tha eye, her ass yelped like a scalded cat. My knuckles throbbed 'cause I threw all my weight behind it. Mavis threw her hands up and backed away. 'That's right boo, you don't want none of dis ass whoopin' I'm deliverin'.' Kelly swung back all wild, tha shit flew ova my shoulder. Maybe she couldn't see cause dat eye was closin' faster than a hoe spread her legs for a trick. "Stupid ass!" I yelled, followed by a knee to the gut. "Yo dumb ass still got blue paint on yo hands!" Another to the chin, which knocked her ass from folded over to standin'. Kelly swung again, missed and grabbed my ponytail. Too bad its detachable boo. That shit came right off, leavin' her with a silly ass look on her face; so I hit her with a four piece just for lookin' like dat. Blood shot out of her nose and mouth, splatterin' my tee. Her ass lucky tha shirt wasn't a favorite or I'd really take it to Kelly's ass. "Taylor! Get off my daughter!" blared in my ears. Rosalie grabbed my arm mid swing usin' my momentum to turn me in her direction. "What are you doin'!? She's a child Taylor! If you've got a problem with mines, bring it to me!" bossed Rosalie; standin' before me in shorts, bra and half a head of braids. Kelly lay moanin', bleedin' at my feet. "Yo bitch ass daughter broke in my shit and poured blue paint ova my furniture; and before you tune up them lyin' ass lips, the evidence is all under her fuckin' nails. Now I don't give two shits how ya'll do it, but my shit better be replaced by the end of the day; cause if you think this bad, just wait." I barked back, then chest bumped her ass. "Whatchu not gone do is stand in my face and threaten mines Taylor. You might pump fear in people out here, but I'm not one." Shocked, I gave Rosalie another look. "Really? Well take dis bit of knowledge so you'll know I'm serious." I said, then kicked her in her pus', socked her in the nose and walked off wit a dust of hands. * Three hours later, I'm sittin' at the kitchen table munchin' on pizza bites when I hear a buncha yellin' and what not. Peekin' out tha window, I see Toni all up in Mavis' face. "Aww shit, round two." I swear these hoes love to keep shit goin'. I'm just sayin'. Slidin' on flip flops, I stepped outside into chaos. A big ass fight was in progress! Weave, someone's wig and extended lashes lay scattered. People were yellin' and some dude jumped in after one girl hit tha ground and lay motionless. Shirts were ripped off puttin' stretchmarks, burn marks, cuts and keloids on display. Blood, slob and a few teeth flew; raggedy bras and holey drawers came into play when two girls were beat out there clothing. Mavis yanked Caren's bra up and over her head, dudes made gaggin' noises at the sight of flapjacks she called tits. 'Ump, dis girl only seventeen and had no kids, so why yo shits lookin' like elephant tits? Shit so saggy she could step on her own titty. One was way bigger than the otha, while the smaller oozed a pus like substance. Another chick had a navel ring; the ring had rust and green shit growin' outta it and was turnin' her outtie navel rainbow colors. Sirens could be heard quickly approachin'. I saw Dove roll up, so side steppin' tha ruckus, I strode over and jumped in the car. Dove grabbed a box of Raisinets and started munchin' away while Bryson Tiller played on the radio. 'Gurll what tha fuck jumped off WWF's Royal Rumble outchere?" Dove asked, eyes all wide. Dis nosy trick always in somebody's business, just messy. 'Not sure. It started between Toni and Mavis." I shrugged, cause all I cared about was seein' a furniture truck roll up wit' my shit. Cops jumped out, yellin' 'cease and desist', which was ignored until they pulled out expandable batons and started wackin' knees and crackin arms until order was somewhat restored. 'Wow, Sincere jus' took off. They aren't catchin' dat mafucka." joked Dove. 'Right. Anyhoo it's Thursday, wanna hit up tha Legion or the Elks?" Dove twisted her lips. "I guess so, ain't like no other clubs jumpin' on a Thursday." "A'ight." I opened the door and got out. "Come scoop me around eleven." Dove frowned. "Eleven? You know clubs close early tonight, we need to be there before that. Shit, I'm tryina leave saucy. You know them old bastards shell out the cash." "Fine, ten and not a minute earlier." Slammin' the door, I saw Toni stridin' in my direction. I hope her ass don't try and do me 'cause she sees a few cops out dis piece; cause I'll still pound her shit to tha white meat and happily skip my black ass to the cruiser. "Uh, Taylor.. can I speak to you for a sec?" Eyebrow arched, I gave the screw face cause whatchu got to say to moi? That I beat cho mom and sister's ass and now you want some too? Or is it you got my money? Or furniture receipt? "What?" Toni pulled a slip of paper out her bra and passed it. I took that shit with two fingers. Did I smell musk? Ooo, dats tha worse when you got breast musk, I'm just sayin'. It was an invoice from Raymour & Flanigan for a couch, loveseat, recliner and table. My eyes slid down to the total, $3500. A smile formed. "Thanks, and when can I expect my furniture?" "Tomorrow afternoon." My smile grew. "Thank Brick for me." Turning, I made my way inside, then called Jacko to come toss this crap for forty bucks. * "Damn, I forgot to tell Tay' 'bout me beatin' up Aisha last night." Dove muttered aloud, wide smile gracing her lips. Hearing the house phone ringing Dove quickly stepped inside and snatched it up. "Hello?" "Bitch! When I see yo ass it's a wrap! You put Aisha in the hospital, she lost my son!" Roared Bernard, harsh breathing assaulting her ear. "Who's this?" Teased Dove, pulling out her last bogie. she lit up deeply inhaled then rolled her eyes. "Fuck you Dove.." "Besides," she cut in. "...you've already got a son, he's at yo moms. Why don't you go see his ass insteada worryin' 'bout a dead fetus; and for tha record, that trick stepped to me and got what her hand called for, a mothafuckin' beat down!" Dove yelled back. she could hear Bernard's teeth grinding. "Yeah, I'll see you shorty and getcho bastard from my momma's!" "What!? Nigga you lunchin', dats his G'ma.." "Hoe please." Bernard said cutting her short. "Dat DNA test I took came back. My momma called me and told me I'm 99.999% not Jeff's father. So hop yo sorry, dick ridin', non cleanin' ass, STD walkin' self to my momma's before I leave dis hospital and set his lil ass on da curb. No more babysitter bitch!" Click. Stunned, Dove stared at the phone in disbelief. Yeah Jeff wasn't his, but never in a million years did she think Bernard would develop the smarts to check on his own. * Dressed casually in Dereon jeans and top and Roman sandals, I jumped in Dove's car and did a double take. Jeff waved hello then said, "Where you hoes goin' tonight?" Woosa Tay' don't climb ova tha seat and serve his lil grown ass. "Nigglet dats none of yo b.i. I'ma grown ass woman.." "I know,"

Jeff licked ashy lips, "and I can't wait to tap dat cause yo man ain't hittin' you right. You too up tight." My jaw dropped, Dove pulled off like she don't hear her man-child comin' at me sideways. Now when I slap his ass off da seat she bet not say shit then either. "Jeff, how old are you?" He smirked. "Old enough. My momma say you like 'em young anyway, so why you playin' shorty?" My head whipped in Dove's direction. Dis trick gone turn up her staticky ass radio. "A'ight, I'll let you have dat Jeff." "Hmp, what else you gone let me have?" He stuck his tongue out and flapped it back and forth. Ooo, dis lil ninja was really tryina take me there! I could feel the switch itchin' to flip. Thankfully Dove pulled over on Tower Avenue, put the car in park and jumped out. "C'mon boy, I don't got all night." she griped. "Who lives here?" I asked, clueless on why we'd stopped before a peach single family house. "Brian and his girl Tiphanie." Slammin' the door, Dove marched up the driveway, Jeff and two suitcases in tow. Before she could knock, the door swung open and there stood Brian. He hadn't changed much. I could see him strainin' to get a good look at who sat in tha front seat and since I wanted no parts, I turned my back, whipped out my cell and jumped on Facebook. Flippin' through some pics, my lips twisted. Ump, some hoes have no damn shame, postin' all their business. Postin' there man's dick size, postin' pics of them in bra and panties; tha shit went on and on. Take an ad out and sell tha pus' why don't you. Mavis had posted a video of the fight which I shared on my page. Shit, next time I gotta kung fu a hoe I'mma have someone film it so I can post it on Girl Fights, Gorilla Fights, Mediatakeout and Bossip; cause dese bitches getting' beside they self and need to be reminded who tha hell I be. I'm just sayin'. Brian started yellin' so I cracked tha window to get my listen on. 'Look Brian, I could give a lion's stankin' pussy on how Tiphanie's gonna feel when she comes home from suckin' d..I mean work. Jeff's yo son and its time he gets to know you! Now either we do this or I'll see yo ass in child support court. Plus, I'll tell everybody how dat trick done brainwashed you and turned you against yo own flesh and blood." She lashed. Brian gasped like a fish outta water for a hot second, before he fully opened the door, allowin' Jeff in and takin' his luggage. Dove strutted down the drive like she was America's Next Top Model. Please, more like America's Top Slut, or the next hoe who thinks her pus' is tha ultimate smorgasbord. I'm just sayin'...

CHAPTER 2

Dove drove past the American Legion which had about ten cars, then decided to see how the Elks fared. They were packed! The parking lot and both sides of a oneway were fulla cars. 'Aww sukey! Hurry up, I see a car leavin' tha lot!" Dove's non drivin' ass rolled up on the curb, cut cross the grass and damn near blocked the Honda leavin' the exit. At the door they were chargin' eight which surprisingly Dove paid for she and I. Inside, every table was full, along with the stools at the bar. People leaned against walls and crowded the dance floor. "Good evening ladies, may I buy you drinks?" Issey Miyake surrounded me. Smilin', I turned and came face to face with dis he-she named Reba. I mean ole gurl had her boobs lopped off and took hormone pills and injections. If you didn't know her before alla this, you'd never know she was a girl until she dropped her boxers. Reba aka Ron was a better lookin' dude. I'm just sayin'. 'Hey Ron." purred Dove with a hug so tight her boobs were smooshed. Ump, some people have no shame I tell ya. I think Dove's ass would fuck a horse if the price was right. Chuckle. 'Hey Dove. Taylor, long time no see." Since Dove wanted the floor, I let her have it. I excused myself and hit up the bar, head bobbin' to the sounds of my bitch Lil Kim. That's my mafuckin' dog right there. I saw her years ago in concert and ever since can't nobody say shit 'bout her while I'm around. YoYo's crazy ass was runnin' tha bar. For a time, she and I were tight; 'til ha dick drove her crazy and she ended up hittin' her ex's new girl with her car, then backed up and ran her over. Ump, dat must've been some good damn dick to make a chick try and kill another with her rental car. That's a lil to much, even for moi. 'Aww do the stanky leg! My homie Taylor in da house!" Screamed YoYo the other bartender, jumped and dropped a Heinken on the floor in surprise. 'Hey YoYo, how's it goin'? Where you been hidin'?" 'Prison. Just got out last year an shit, tryin' to get the twins back. Sup wit' you?" I shrugged. 'Same shit, different tissue. Let me get a Sex on the beach. Nah, let me get a Snakebite." YoYo wiggled her bushy brows. 'Girl, member when we'd drink dem shits, den hit tha club? Whoo those was some good times!" 'Damn! Can you stop reminiscing and make my damn drank!? You wanna flashback, flashback on all da pus' you ate and mop handles up yo snatch, fuck outta here! Reminisce on how yo ass

got ten years wit' a mandatory eight and two of probation."
"Yeah, those were the days alright." YoYo finally passed me my
shit, told me it was on the house, winked, licked her lips and
served the next waitin' customer; givin' me a chance to fully take
her in. Once slim, YoYo was damn near as wide as a deep freezer.
Where she wouldn't be caught dead without make-up and fresh
hairdo, her face was plain, not even lip gloss adorned crunchy
lips; and she'd cut off full, shoulder length locks and now sported
a small afro. See what a dick a do to you. Weak bitches, I swear.
The DJ threw on another oldie, Blaque's 808 and the dance
floor swelled with couples. I could see Dove and Reba cuttin' a
rug, that's right, I said Reba. She ain't no damn Ron if a penis
ain't swingin' between her legs to prove it. 'Wanna dance?" Hot
ass, liquored breath fried my nape hairs. 'Fuck, I ain't in the
mood for no b.s.' Turnin', face all twisted, I glared at dude
before me. High yellow, face full of freckles, a big wide nose and
large booty eatin' lips. 'Lips so big he smiles and wets his hair.
Lips so big he needs a paintbrush to swipe on Chapstick.' I'm
just sayin'. 'No thanks, I'm jus' chillin'." I started to say maybe
lata, but why lie; I wasn't dancin' wit' dude now or later,
somethin' 'bout his ass rubbed me tha wrong damn way. Kinda
like when you rub yo pet so hard they snap at cho ass. Openin'
my purse, I pulled out a cigarette and a pair of brass knuckles. As
I've said before, yo girl stays ready fo' da bullshit. 'What? Hoe

don't get beside yo'self, it's just a dance. You ain't all dat!" Spittle flew, landin' on my hand. Nasty bastard; the switch jiggled. 'Uh hunh, well then gone 'bout yours and ask someone else to dance." Dude weaved on his feet while his eyes rolled like he had no control over their muscles. 'Don't..you..hoe I said let's dance, or you gone have problems!" Suddenly he grabbed my arm hard while pullin' me off the stool. I knocked over my Snakebite. 'Nucca, dat liquor done made you fuck wit' tha right one!" I blasted and came up swingin'. he stumbled from the blow while blood dribbled under his right eye. Dats right, the switch was all the way up, so far dat mafucka was stuck. Dude roared like a wounded grizzly, raised a hand and cupped bloody face. 'You. You h..hit me." he slurred. Being that it was so packed, security couldn't see what had popped off, so I jabbed his shocked ass twice more before some chick saw what was goin' on and started chantin'; 'Security, security to the dance floor!" Dove came runnin' behind security, took one look at dude on the floor rollin' and moanin' like he took a bullet to the gut and burst out laughing. 'Tay' why you beatin' up Guy? Yo ass crazy!" She bellowed. Hands on hips, I glared between the two. 'Guy? Who the fuck is Guy!?" Dove giggled. 'Dats Marcus' step daddy girl. He saw me on tha dance floor, asked if I wanted a drink. I tol' him hell yeah and to buy my girl Tay one too." She looked down, watching the two bouncers help Guy up. 'Jeez his cheekbones swellin' somethin' serious, you might've broke his joint." Shrug. 'Cause I don't car either way. Plus, tha drunk bastard didn't ask if I wanted a drink, he got all up in my space actin' all ignant, so he got what his hand called for. "Whateva." Lip smack. "Guy spilled my shit. You sent dat drunk fool ova here, so dig in dat grungy bra, pull out sum green and get me anotha." I ordered. 'Was dis chick fo' real?' thought Dove. 'How am I responsible cause she wildin' out? Suddenly I really want dis hoe to suffer.' Pulling a wrinkled twenty from bra, Dove squeezed in at the bar, flagged down some butch lookin' chick and ordered herself a Rum Punch and Tay's Snakebite, Dove had half a mind to accidently on purpose knock said drink dead in her lap. "Here you lush." Taylor snatched her drink then smirked. "So where's yo boyfriend? Y'all were all hugged up and swappin' spit." Dove chuckled. "Oh, you saw that hunh?" "Hmm, what's up with you Dove? One minute you on dick and tha next you bumpin' twats?" Dove sipped her drink, winked and walked off. *

CHAPTER 3

"Yo Dove, hol' up!" Just about to jump in her car to go check on Jeff, she was halted by Kione's fione self. Sultry smile in place, Dove closed the door, then leaned against it. "Hey stranger. Where you been hiding witcho cute self?" Kione walked up so close their knees collided. Dove's eyes widened in surprise at the move. 'I had some shit to take care of but I'm back now. So what's up ma?" 'Wait...what? Did I hear that shit right?' Dove silently questioned, ready to take it as far as Kione was willing to go. 'Fuck, I wanted him first.' her thoughts continued. "Wateva, you want to be is up." Kione smiled and leaned in for a quick smooch. 'Damn, his ass tastes like melted chocolate.' she ruminated. "Why don't we hook up later at my place?" Dove asked. Kione cupped her breast and ran a thumb over distended nipple. "Yo joint harder than stone, got a nigga mouthwatering and shit." "Oh yeah? Well I can definitely help you with that." She purred, pussy juicing from nipple stimulation. "What time you wanna see dis big dick?" Mouth drying, Dove wiggled a lil bit and felt nothin' but heat and hardness pressed against her. Pictures of Kione's dick in her mouth, her tongue up firm cheeks, had her knees trembling. 'Wait..what had he asked her? Oh yeah, what time.' Mused Dove. "Um, midnight." Kione smiled. "A'ight, midnight it is. Be ready fo' a hella workout." Kione tweaked her nipple, forcing a moan from parted panting lips. "See you lata shorty." Dove watched him depart, thoughts of riding what felt like ten inches stewing, only for Taylor to impede her thoughts. 'Hmm, how would Taylor feel once she found out Kione's dick held her pussy juices?'Another thought slid in. What if she caught them in the act? After all, Taylor had done her wrong on numerous occasions. She always had some slick shit to say and she'd had her kidnapped for her own sick ass reasons; so a lil payback was definitely in order. Pleased smirk on her face, Dove opened the car door and jumped in. * "Bitch! I'm here to check on my son! Not to stand here debatin' wit' yo ugly insecure ass!" barked Dove. For the past ten minutes she'd stood ringing Brian's doorbell, only for the curtains to flutter. So Dove kept her finger on the bell until Tiphanie finally yanked it open with a dumb look plastered on her face. "Where's Jeff?" demanded Dove, eyes trying to see around Tiphanie's wide frame. "I don't appreciate you popping up at my home, that's what phones are for.."

'Listen fatty," Dove cut in. 'I give zero fucks about how you feel. I came to check on mines, so go get his ass or get out the damn way!" She barked again. Tiphanie, who felt self-conscious about her weight, flushed a deep red at the insult. 'I beg your pardon? How dare you! So what I'm a little overweight. Brian doesn't complain when I ride him, so take your bony, insult having ass away from my home this instant!" Tiphanie screamed back, breathing erratic. She tried to calm down before an asthma attack had her visiting the E.R. again. Dove laughed. 'Yo half breed ass don't even know how to cuss." she chuckled again. 'And fo' tha record Hefty cinch sack, I'm totally grossed out from the thought of yo ass ridin' anythin'; especially Brian's sexy ass." Tiphanie's eyes watered, seein' it Dove went in for the kill. 'Hmp." she smacked her lips like she'd just finished a four piece from Kfc. 'I can still remember suckin' dat dick. Does he still shiver when you stick yo tongue in tha slit? Does he still like doggy style the best?" Dove moaned. 'and the way dat mafucka eats da pus' should be against tha law. Anyway, I've taken up enough of your time. I don't see Brian's car, so I'll stop by the barber shop. Ta ta." sang Dove, as she turned and strode back to her car. * Shop Rite was packed and it wasn't even check day. Normally I shopped at Stop N Shop, but because I had a buy one, get one free coupon for a bag of whiting for Shop Rite, I took a drive out to Wethersfield; which was the closest. I'd invited Joshua over for dinner tomorrow and with nothing in my freezer, so to the store I went. Grabbing a cart, I started over by the lettuce and tomatoes, ignoring hateful glares from a few white people. As long as they stayed in their lane, the switch wouldn't flip on they ass. I'm just saying. Pickin' up a pack of ribs, I felt someone starin' hard as fuck. Refusin' to look around, I left the meats and went up the cereal aisle; yo gurl loved some Honeycomb cereal. Pickin' up two boxes, I hit the next aisle and hear, "Taylor! What a coincidence seeing you here. I've called and texted you numerous times, but you never answered. Did your number change or something?" I knew dat irritating ass voice anywhere. Glancing up, there he was, ole Brandon from the club. He wore boat shoes and Bermuda shorts with a tee that read, 'Single looking to mingle!' Corny ass. With a huff, I gave a dry ass, "Sup." and started to push my cart when dis ninja grabbed it. "You were right. About going black and never going back. I miss you Taylor. I hope you feel the same now that fate's brought us together." Was dis fool for real? Was I bein' punked? Crazy shone brightly from his eyes, like a beacon on a stormy night. The switch jiggled. "Dats nice and all, but I'm busy. See you around." I told him. Not if I could help it. I swear, you fuck a mafucka one time and they think they own yo ass; crazy stalkin' bastard. Brandon reached out and grabbed my arm. Oh no he didn't! Switch on, I let him have a slice of get right. "First off, don't touch me unless fuckin' invited!" I snapped all loud. A few custies in the aisle gave a look, while a Hispanic girl pulled out her cell and started recording. 'Second, buy a clue. If I don't answer yo calls and texts, that means kick rocks, I ain't interested. Now unless you got two g's in yo pocket, ain't shit else to discuss!" A hurt look slid over his face like tha shit was supposed to fuckin' faze me. Please, money talks and bullshit runs a marathon. I'm just sayin'. Before I could really go ham, some heavyset florid faced white man with a badge that read, manager Oscar Martin, hurried towards us. 'Sir, is this young lady harassing you? It was brought to my attention there was a disturbance." He turned watery green eyes on me. 'Young lady, here at Shop Rite we do not condone harassment or solicitation of our customers of any type." he faced Brandon. 'Sir if you'd like, I can detain her while I call the police." See. His ass threatenin' a bitch with the law. Hunny chile call dem sons of bitches, cause Taylor James always has bond money okay! 'Listen you fat, sweaty faced, racist bastard. If yo ass put down the snack long enough to have checked tha security tapes before speed walkin' ova here accusin' me of bullshit, you would've saw me mindin' mines and dis asshole followin' and harassin' me. So call tha fuckin' po-po and when they get here and I raise so much hell they'll have no choice but to view 'em, then release me, I'll call every news channel and a damn good lawyer to sue you and dis fuckin' store!" Oscar glanced at Brandon, only to find he no longer stood there; his hand held green basket the only proof that he'd been there at all. "Um, I..I'm so sorry for the misunderstanding Ms.?" I kept quiet, switch all tha way turnt the hell up. "Yes..well," he cleared his throat. "There's no need to take things that far ma'am. I'm sure we can come to some sort of arrangement." My brows arched. "I'm listenin'." "How about a one-hundred-dollar gift card?" He pleaded. With holdin' a grin, I pretended to ponder over Oscar's words. "Uhm, I don't know. I've never been so embarrassed...." "Three hundred." Oscar hastily threw out. I glanced at my cart two boxes of cereal and a pack of ribs. "Throw in my groceries and we have a deal." "Done." Needless to say, I walked outta Shop Rite with three-hundred-dollar gift card and four hundred and seventy five dollars' worth of free groceries. *

ABOUT
THE AUTHOR

New York Times & International Best Selling Author Billie
Dureyea Shell was born in Compton California and now lives
in Ladera Heights with his wife and
kids who he loves to spend time with.
He is the Owner of several properties in the Los Angeles area
and gives back to his community by providing low income
housing to those who need it.
He stated "It doesn't matter where you at or where you from
it's what you do with your time. There's nothing you can't do
if you put your mind to it".

Lightning Source UK Ltd.
Milton Keynes UK
UKHW020630150721
387203UK00005B/39